Jackie Ashenden writes dark, emotional stories with alpha heroes who've just got the world to their liking only to have it blown wide apart by their kick-ass heroines. She lives in Auckland, New Zealand, with her husband, the inimitable Dr Jax, two kids and two rats. When she's not torturing alpha males and their gutsy heroines she can be found drinking chocolate martinis, reading anything she can lay her hands on, wasting time on social media, or being forced to go mountain biking with her husband.

To keep up to date with Jackie's new releases and other news you can sign up to her newsletter at jackieashenden.com.

If you liked *Destroyed*, why not try

Ruined by Jackie Ashenden
Make Me Crave by Katee Robert
Wild Thing by Nicola Marsh
Best Laid Plans by Rebecca Hunter

Discover more at millsandboon.co.uk

DESTROYED

JACKIE ASHENDEN

This book is produced from independently certified FSC™ paper to ensure responsible forest management.

For more information visit www.harpercollins.co.uk/green.

Printed and bound in Spain
by CPI, Barcelona

MILLS & BOON

First Published in Great Britain 2018
by Mills & Boon, an imprint of HarperCollins*Publishers*
1 London Bridge Street, London, SE1 9GF

© 2018 Jackie Ashenden

ISBN: 978-0-263-93226-3

This one's for all the lovely editors at the
Mills & Boon UK office who've worked with me
over the years.

It took me a while, guys, but I got there in the end!

CHAPTER ONE

Summer

BRAVERY WAS NEVER my strong suit, but I guess it takes a certain amount of courage to talk your way into a biker's bedroom in an outlaw motorcycle club's clubhouse purely so you can hide from your father.

Either that or I was simply stupid, difficult as that was to admit for a person with an IQ score over 170.

Whatever it was, as I sat on Crash's bed in his tiny squalid bedroom, my heart racing, listening to the sounds of a heavy driving beat and male laughter going on outside, I was beginning to question my decision big time.

Two doors separated the bedrooms from the main living area of the clubhouse, but the bikers were so freaking loud I could still hear whatever was going on outside. I didn't know whether it was a party or what—I'd only ever been in the clubhouse a couple of times before—but whatever it was, it didn't make me any less nervous.

Crash had left me in his room, muttering something about why don't I relax while he went and got us some beers.

I didn't really want a beer—I wasn't a party girl and I didn't like alcohol—but sitting on Crash's bed, listening to those sounds outside the door, made the idea of some liquid courage not half-bad.

Especially since he'd been gone awhile and my anxiousness was starting to tip over into outright fear.

His room was little more than a closet, the floor covered with dirty clothes and beer cans and all kinds of other things I didn't want to look at too closely. The bed I was sitting on was unmade and there was a smell to the air that reminded me of my older brother Justin's room when he was younger. Sweaty teenage boy, musty and a bit rank. It was unpleasant and made me feel sick.

I wiped my damp palms nervously on my denim mini.

Okay, maybe it really *had* been stupid to come here. Then again, I hadn't known where else to go. I'd been dumb enough to tell Dad about my Silicon Valley job offer, hoping he'd be happy for me, but of course he hadn't been.

He'd told me I wasn't going and that was final, and that he'd do whatever it took to make me stay here in Brooklyn with him.

I knew what 'whatever it took' meant. Emotional manipulation, emotional blackmail, and if I was really unlucky, he might stoop to physical restraint, too. Dad had always hated being told no.

The quiet and introverted teen I'd once been

would have automatically bowed her head and agreed with him. But I'd just come back from three years at college and the time away from him had allowed me some breathing room. I'd had space to grow, to realise that there was a better life out there, one that wasn't constantly overshadowed by his presence.

Sure, I was still quiet and introverted, but when he'd told me I couldn't go, I discovered I had a bit of backbone after all.

I couldn't let him take my dream job away from me. I couldn't let him stop me from trying to live my life. My ticket was booked and I'd be out of here in a couple of days. All I had to do was avoid him so he couldn't do his usual emotional number on me and get me to change my mind.

It would have been fine if I'd been a stronger sort of person, but I wasn't. He always found my vulnerable spots and used them against me, just like the bullies in school used to. I knew I was weak so it was better I take myself out of the equation. Go somewhere he'd never think to find me, never in a million years.

The Knights of Ruin MC's clubhouse.

As police chief, my dad had had a few run-ins with the Knights in the past, though these days he was best buddies with Keep, the Knights' president. Dad would never expect me to have run here, not to the most notorious MC in the state, and especially not when Keep would give me up to him first chance he got if I was ever discovered here.

Which was why I'd come in disguise, dressing up the way I'd seen other girls who wanted a walk on the wild side with a bunch of outlaw bikers do—tiny denim miniskirt and stilettos, a tight blue crop top. I'd had to kill the effect by putting a hoodie on over the top, with the hood pulled up, but I couldn't afford for anyone to see my face. Not that anyone would recognise me these days, but still. Better safe than sorry.

Getting in had been a problem. The only biker whose name I could remember—other than Keep—was Tiger. He'd once been my bodyguard for a month back when I was in high school and I still remembered him. I could hardly forget him, truth be told, so his name had been the first on my lips when I'd been interrogated by the prospect at the door. Unfortunately, though, Tiger was 'busy' and so I'd had to think fast and make up some other lie.

I wasn't experienced with men, had no idea that perhaps flashing my tits would have worked better, but luckily at that moment a semifamiliar face had appeared. I'd met Crash only a couple of times, in conjunction with Tiger, and had no idea if he'd remember me or not. I threw myself at him anyway, begging him to let me inside and that I'd make it worth his while.

He grabbed me around the waist and grinned at the prospect, and before I knew it I'd been bundled down the corridor and into his bedroom.

Unfortunately, I was starting to think that not only had I been stupid to come here, I'd been naive into the bargain. There were stories about the Knights that I'd heard from various friends, about drunken parties and public sex and threesomes and all kinds of things.

And now I was in the thick of it.

Alone.

So much for my high IQ. Panic had made me stupid. Again.

More sounds came from outside the door. A man shouting and then the sounds of a scuffle followed by laughter. Something thumped hard against the wall and I jumped in shock.

God, I wasn't cut out for this.

I was just starting to wonder if I could slip right back out again without anyone noticing when the door banged open and Crash came in. He was a good-looking guy, which made me nervous since good-looking guys always did. Actually, men in general made me nervous, good-looking or otherwise.

You sure picked the wrong place to hide then, didn't you?

Given that the clubhouse was full of men, violent and loud, yeah, it really had been.

'Still here?' he asked, grinning and swaying on his feet.

I decided not to tell him that he was stating the obvious since men generally didn't like it when I did that, settling for smoothing my miniskirt instead and trying to smile.

Okay, so I was naive. But I wasn't *that* naive. I knew what girls in MC clubhouses were supposed to do and I knew that Crash hadn't brought me into his bedroom because he wanted to chat about the finer points of game theory—my favourite subject. He'd brought me here because he thought I was ready for some hot sex.

As if on cue, he sauntered over from the door, two beers in his hand, then held one out to me. That grin was still on his face and there was a glazed look in his blue eyes. As he stood there swaying, I finally realised what I should have known the moment he'd grabbed me and hustled me into his bedroom: Crash was drunk. Very, very drunk.

Dammit.

Drunk guys were always super fun. *Not*.

I took the beer, the can cold against my damp palm, and tried to resist the urge to do something about my fear by downing the whole thing in one go.

'So-o-o-o…' Crash said slowly, lifting his own beer and taking a swig. 'How long exactly are you planning on keeping your clothes on?'

My palms got even damper and I could feel myself begin to sweat.

Sex. I knew that was what he expected, but… Well, my great plan had kind of ended with me at the clubrooms. I hadn't thought about what I might have to do to *stay* in the clubrooms.

So, is losing your virginity to some guy you barely know in a dirty biker clubhouse really worth avoiding your father for?

That was a very good question. And one I didn't want to find out the answer to. Maybe if I told him I only wanted to hide out here for a while, he'd let me?

I cleared my throat, trying to get the words out. 'I…um…well…there's kind of a reason.'

'Uh-huh.' Crash sat down heavily next to me on

the bed, making me aware of him in a way I didn't like. He was in the usual biker uniform of jeans, a T-shirt and the leather vest they called a 'cut' worn over the top, and I could feel the heat of his body next to mine. He wore a lot of aftershave and that combined with the reek of alcohol coming off him made me want to cringe. 'If that reason is to suck my cock, then, baby, I'm here for that.'

Fear fluttered in my gut.

Yeah, I didn't want to do that. Even the thought of it made me feel ill. I'd never done it before and I certainly didn't want to start with some drunken biker, just because I'd apparently lost my mind and made a decision that was, in retrospect, looking to be the stupidest decision in the history of creation.

'W-what if it's…not that?' I asked hesitantly.

'Oh, come on…' He leaned in, nuzzling against my ear, his beer breath wafting over me, deepening my discomfort with the whole situation. 'Uh…what did you say your name was again?'

I hadn't told him, and what's more, I couldn't. Because although he might not have known who Summer Grant was, I was pretty sure he was familiar with Campbell Grant, the police chief and my dad. Not that he'd necessarily draw a link between the names, at least not in his current state, but I couldn't risk it.

Desperately I tried to think of another name I could give him, but for once my dumb brain was empty. 'Do you really need to know that?'

He left a wet kiss beneath my ear that made my

skin crawl. 'Nah. Couldn't give a shit. Just gimme a taste of that pussy.'

I cringed again, both at the crass way he was talking and at how he was leaning over me. 'Hey.' I tried to pull away from him. 'What would you say if I…uh…didn't want to have sex with you?'

He gave a drunken laugh, reaching for my hand. 'Are you kidding me? Then what the hell am I supposed to do with this?' And he pressed my hand right down over his fly, where I could feel him already as hard as a rock.

Wonderful. This situation was getting better and better.

I swallowed, my mouth dry, trying to resist the urge to jerk my hand away since I was pretty sure that would offend him and I didn't want to risk that, not when I wasn't sure what he'd do.

Instead, I left my hand there for a second, then carefully drew it back. 'That's, um…very impressive.' I took a quick sip of my beer, grabbing a bit of that liquid courage and trying not to pull a face at the taste. 'But maybe you could get someone else to do something about it?'

He shook his head and put a hand on my knee, sliding it up to the hem of my skirt. 'Oh, no, baby. It's a party and you're the one in my room. You know what that means.'

I shifted my leg away, attempting to put some distance between us. 'No. I have no idea what that means.' Because, although I knew what it was that he wanted, I didn't know how it being a party made any difference.

Outside, the thumping of the music had increased in volume, and there was lots of loud shouting and laughter. More immediate were the rhythmic noises coming from the room next door and someone moaning, while someone else cursed.

I could feel my face flushing.

'Well,' Crash mumbled, trying to slide his fingers beneath my skirt yet again. 'Girls only go into a brother's room for one reason and here's a hint. It's not to chat.'

I knew that. Of course I knew that.

But you didn't think it through first so now you have to deal.

My heart shuddered in my chest, the fear inside me getting wider, deeper. Would he even let me go if I didn't want to have sex with him? And if I got out of Crash's room, what would happen then? I'd have to run the gauntlet of those men outside all the way back to the entrance of the club.

Yeah, you're a freaking genius. Mensa would love to have you. Not.

I shivered, feeling like the biggest fool to ever draw breath. What had I been thinking? I hadn't; that was my problem. I'd let my anger at Dad and at my own weakness get the better of me, and now I was here, being pressured into having sex with a drunken biker.

Awesome.

I pushed Crash's hand away yet again, trying frantically to think of a solution to this particular problem. But sadly this was real life and it wasn't quite as simple as a math equation. There were no rules I could apply here and way too many variables, and when you were battling panic, logic didn't always work.

'C-can't we chat?' I wriggled away from him. 'Just while I finish my beer?'

But his hand was now sliding underneath my hoodie, over my bare stomach, and he was pulling me very close, his mouth at my neck. 'Nah. I don't wanna chat. C'mon, baby. Put those lips to work.'

I went rigid, my heart now climbing up into my throat. I could feel the strength in his arm going around me. I knew I couldn't fight it.

Men, they were all the same. Even the ones who were supposed to be the good guys were assholes, and I knew that better than anyone.

In the corridor outside, a woman giggled, the deep voice of a man saying something in return.

'Well, o-okay.' I hated the way I couldn't keep my voice from shaking. 'But I'm a virgin, you know that, right?' It had been my experience that once you said the 'V' word, men usually ran for the hills.

Sadly Crash didn't run, though to be fair, there were no hills he could logically run to.

'Mmm…' he said. 'Then maybe I can teach you.' And he moved his hand up to cup my breast.

I don't know what happened then. Something in me simply snapped, roaring in negation as his hand cupped me, and I found myself shoving him away hard before I could think better of it, yelling 'No' as loud as I could for good measure.

Then, as I was sitting there, trembling with anger and fear, the door to Crash's room burst open with such force that it bounced back against the wall with a bang.

A man was standing in the doorway. A horribly familiar man.

'What the fuck is going on?' the man demanded, his voice deep and dark, rough and gritty. Then his strange amber eyes met mine and my heart clenched tight with a weird combination of absolute terror and utter relief.

Jake Clarke, aka Tiger.

I'd never forgotten the first day I'd met him. He'd been waiting for me outside my school one day, sitting astride his massive black Harley and smoking a cigarette. He'd worn battered blue jeans, a black T-shirt with a leather vest thrown over the top, and there were chains attached to his belt, huge motorcycle boots on his feet, brightly coloured tattoos wrapping around both his powerful arms.

He was as beautiful as the animal he was named for and twice as dangerous. Mean as hell and sexy as sin.

The sun had struck copper sparks from his dark hair, and when he'd seen that school was out, he'd thrown his cigarette down right there in the street and ground it under his heel. Then he'd looked straight at me.

And I'd forgotten where I was. I'd even forgotten who I was.

His eyes were amber, the colour of expensive whisky or newly minted gold coins, and they had pinned me to the spot. A golden arrow straight through my heart.

His face was all hard lines and arrogant angles, his brows slightly winged at the corners, and he had the hardest, sharpest jawline I'd ever seen. He didn't smile. His mouth was wide and beautifully carved, and the rounded shape of his bottom lip was the softest part about him, but it didn't curve.

All my friends had stared at him—hell, *everyone* had stared at him. No one in my exclusive girls' school had ever seen a man like him.

'There'll be someone there to meet you after school today,' Dad had told me that morning. 'In fact, he'll be taking you to and from school for a little while so be nice to him, okay?'

Tiger had been that someone. An enforcer for the Knights of Ruin MC, he'd been assigned to be my bodyguard to protect me from the death threats another MC had thrown at my father. And Dad, being canny, had decided that the best protection from one MC was a rival MC.

I'd been terrified of Tiger and excited by him in equal measure, and I'd fallen in love with him the moment I'd seen him. But back then I was only seventeen and a nerdy, tongue-tied little girl, while he was twenty-six and a full-grown man, and so far out of my league he might as well have been the sun to my Pluto.

He was a star while I…I was barely even a planet.

It had taken me years to get him out of my head and I'd thought I'd managed it while I'd been away at college. But one look at him was all it took for those feelings to come flooding back. The fear and the curiosity and the dry-mouthed excitement.

I'd thought my situation couldn't get any worse.

I was wrong.

CHAPTER TWO

Tiger

THE SIGHT OF the girl sitting on Crash's bed, staring at me with the biggest, deepest blue eyes I'd ever seen, hit me like a fucking brick to the head.

Not only because she was as white as a goddamn sheet, but also because I knew her.

Summer Grant. Daughter of that well-known asshole Campbell Grant, the police chief.

What the ever-loving fuck was she doing here?

I'd been enjoying the party, aka the usual Saturday night at the clubhouse, and had gone off to spend a little quality time with Mercy, one of the club girls, and hadn't been in the mood to hear some girl shout 'No' from behind a closed bedroom door, and still less to do anything about it.

But I didn't have much patience with brothers who didn't treat the girls right, so I'd kicked the door open to check out what was going on, to make sure things were okay. Only to find Summer fucking Grant sitting there, shaking, on the bed with that dumbass Crash trying to get his hands all over her.

The brother was drunk as a fucking skunk and didn't appear to notice that his door was currently hanging off its hinges. Or that I was standing there. Or even that I'd asked him a goddamn question.

He reached again for the police chief's pretty little daughter.

Fuck. No.

I took two steps into the room, grabbed Crash by his collar, jerked him off the bed, then shoved him up against the wall. 'You hurt her?' I demanded, gripping him by the throat. 'Say yes and I'll punch your fucking face in.'

Couldn't have brothers hurting the girls here. Made for a bad rep and brought trouble, and if there was one thing the Knights didn't need right now it was trouble.

Crash blinked at me, choking slightly in my hold. 'No,' he managed to get out, but I gave him a cuff over the face all the same, because he was an asshole and needed to learn a lesson.

I took my hand away and left him to drop in a heap on the floor, then I turned around to see how Summer was doing.

She was sitting on the bed, giving me big eyes and fear and not saying a fucking word.

'Want to tell me what you're doing here, baby?' I asked her.

Crash croaked something from the floor, but I stuck my boot in his gut as a warning. 'Didn't ask you, dumbass.' This time he must have found some brains from somewhere because he closed his mouth again pretty quickly.

Summer still didn't say a word, hunching over and looking down at her hands like they were the most fascinating things she'd ever seen her life.

Fuck. Looked like my evening of beer, a smoke and a couple of relaxing blow jobs was toast.

'Summer,' I said, keeping things mild because it was clear she was shit-scared, 'let's start again from the top. What the fuck are you doing here?'

At that point there came a loud burst of noise from the corridor outside and I glanced towards the doorway, catching a glimpse of some shrieking girls and a couple of the brothers laughing as they all came in from the living area, obviously in search of some bedrooms.

Mercy, hanging around by the broken door, gave me a pointed look.

Christ. I needed to lock this shit down before someone going past got a look at Summer and recognised her, and started wondering what the hell the police chief's daughter was doing hanging around the clubhouse.

'Sorry, Merc.' I gestured to the girl on the bed, who was hunching her shoulders and generally trying to make herself invisible. A bit of an impossibility when she was wearing a miniskirt that barely covered her pussy and left a pair of long slender legs very, very bare. 'Got a situation I have to handle. Maybe we'll have some fun later.'

And I *did* have to handle it. If Summer decided to make a complaint about Crash to her dad, things could go badly for the Knights. We'd already had some drama with the chief's son and we did not need any more with his daughter.

Mercy made a pouty face, but she was a good girl who knew when to back off. 'Yeah, okay, but I'm holding you to that.'

I didn't look after her as she disappeared back down the corridor. Instead, I took a step over to where Summer was sitting with her head bowed. Crash made another sound, but I didn't want to hear it, especially not from him. 'Shut the fuck up,' I warned him, not even bothering to look at him. 'You try forcing a girl again and I won't just punch you in the face. I'll cut off your cock and make you suck it. Understand?'

He didn't say anything, which was just as well since my evening was starting to look less like blow jobs and beer and more like complicated bullshit.

Annoyed, I kicked aside the clothing lying across the floor and came over to the bed where Summer was sitting. 'Baby,' I said again, 'talk to me.'

But she just shook her head and hunched her shoulders even more.

It made me remember when I used to bodyguard for her. She'd been a little scaredy-cat even then, perpetually treating me like I'd frighten her to death if I even looked at her funny.

What was she doing here? And what had Crash done to her to scare her like this?

I crouched in front of her and reached out to grab one of her hands. Her fingers were icy in mine. 'Hey.' I tried to keep my voice gentle, which was difficult since I wasn't a gentle guy by any stretch of the imagination. 'You okay?'

A brother's voice sounded from close to the doorway. Big Red, the VP, from the sounds of things.

Jesus, I really needed to get her out of here.

I rose to my feet and carefully pulled Summer off the bed so she was standing in front of me, her hand still cold in mine.

Her chin came up, her eyes blinking in shock, her hoodie falling back a little, giving me a better look at her face. Yeah, I remembered her all right. Couldn't forget eyes that blue, or that huge and dark. They seemed black beneath her fair, almost colourless brows, and then there was that determined, pointed chin. I remembered trying to tease her out of her constant terrified silence a couple of times, a tactic that had never worked. But that chin of hers used to jut in a way that made me wonder if she wasn't as scared as she seemed, more like pissed instead. And then there was her luscious mouth, all soft and pink and pouty...

Something punched me hard, right in the gut, and since it was pretty much the last thing I expected to feel when looking at Summer Grant, it took me a second to realise that my cock, the impatient motherfucker, was very, *very* interested in that mouth.

Fuck. This was all I needed. Getting inexplicably hard for Campbell Grant's daughter, which was so not happening. Jesus Christ, I'd be lucky if Keep didn't kick my ass from here to fucking Florida if he ever found out.

Not that I'd do anything about it. I hadn't been into

jailbait back when she'd been seventeen and I wasn't into it now. Though I guessed she wasn't seventeen any more. More like…twenty-two maybe? Except she didn't look it, not with those big, frightened eyes. She looked like a kid who'd just woken up from a really bad nightmare.

I didn't mind a bit of fear to get a chick turned on, as long as she was into it. But if she wasn't, then neither was I, and as for outright terror… Yeah, that wasn't hot as far as I was concerned and it pretty much killed the burgeoning hard-on in my jeans. Good fucking job.

'Come on,' I told her, impatient now to get this mess sorted out. 'Party's over.'

I began to move back to the doorway, pulling her with me, but she'd gone rigid, freezing like a block of wood, staring at me like I was some kind of serial killer.

Christ. Please don't tell me I was going to have to haul a terrified girl through the clubhouse in the middle of a party. Knowing my fucking luck, she'd start screaming and then the shit *would* hit the fan. Especially if Keep spotted me and got the wrong idea.

Yeah, that wasn't happening. Except the problem was that I didn't have time to calm her down now, not with a whole lot of brothers out in the corridor. I needed to get her somewhere private, then maybe get her to quit being so scared and tell me what the hell she was doing here. If it was to take a walk on the wild side with some bikers—which a lot of girls did—then I needed to point out what a stupid fucking idea that was. And then I'd tell her exactly what it meant for the club to have the chief of police's daughter found screaming in a brother's bedroom.

If she didn't want to bang a whole bunch of bikers—and quite frankly, given the look on her face right now, I guessed she probably didn't—then I needed to find out what the hell else had brought her there, then take it to Keep for the same reason.

Protecting the club. That was my job and I took it very, very seriously indeed.

'You gonna come with me?' I asked, giving her a chance to move under her own steam.

But she just stared at me, her face completely white, trembling like a leaf.

Shit. She was panicking now and that was another thing I remembered from my time as her protection. There'd only been one instance of trouble and it hadn't been from the MC who'd delivered the death threats, but from some kids at her school. She'd been late meeting me so I'd gone to see where she was, only to find her being bullied outside some classrooms. All it had taken was a hard stare and a couple of threats, and those bitches had run away, but Summer had stood there stock-still, like a deer caught in the headlights of a car. Too afraid to move.

It had taken a lot of coaxing to get her to snap out of it then, but time was something I didn't have right now. Plus, I was an impatient motherfucker, just like my cock. I wanted this over and done with and I wanted it now.

So I put my hands on her hips, picked her up and threw her over my shoulder.

Summer didn't make a sound or even struggle, though I felt every inch of her go rigid.

'Don't scream,' I told her, wrapping my arm around her slender thighs to hold her steady as I turned towards the door. 'I'm not going to hurt you.'

She was completely silent, stiff as a board as I stepped out of Crash's room and into the corridor.

And into the middle of a goddamn orgy.

Great. Something else I was missing out on. Shit.

I tried to ignore all the hot sex happening right in front of me, heading towards my room since that was the only place I could guarantee we wouldn't be interrupted by douchebags.

But, of course, walking down the corridor with a woman thrown over my shoulder wasn't going to go ignored.

Sure enough, as I went past a brother getting head from two different women, he called out something about my 'friend' and that it was rude not to introduce her.

It was going to look unusual for me *not* to join in since it was well known that I was a big fan of the orgy, but since I was damn sure that the pretty little thing over my shoulder wouldn't be thrilled if I suddenly started insisting on her getting to know the brothers and their cocks, I merely gave him the finger and strode on past.

My room was down the corridor a way, and I stopped outside it, my arm still wrapped around her thighs. She was taller than I'd expected and on the skinny side—I preferred chicks with a little more to hold on to—and I was weirdly conscious of the way she smelled, sweet and flowery and kind of innocent. It got to me, that scent. Not sure why, but it did. The club girls I was used to didn't smell like that and I wasn't sure I liked it.

It made me aware of how scared she'd been and of how I was now hauling her around over my shoulder like a sack of coal. Made me wonder if that really had been the best course of action, since it probably wouldn't have helped her fear.

Then I realised what I was doing and glared at my door. What the fuck? I wasn't used to questioning my decisions and I didn't appreciate the fact that I was questioning them now, and all because of the way some scared little girl smelled.

Holy shit. I was going soft.

Irritated with myself, I opened the door and stepped inside.

I actually had a place of my own, but I liked to keep a room at the club because I liked being where my brothers were, where I could get all the cold beer and hot pussy I could handle without having to do a thing.

I wasn't a loner, unlike my buddy Smoke. I liked people. I liked a party, too, lots of music, alcohol and women… Everything a man needed to feel good, and since feeling good was my preferred state, I indulged myself often.

Pity I was missing out on all of that now, though, which was pissing me off. Especially after the day I'd had taking care of some Demon's Share MC assholes who'd accidentally-on-purpose wandered into our territory and had needed a little reminder to stay out of it.

Anyway, I'd been looking forward to some R & R tonight, a chance to forget about my problems for a little while, but now I had to deal with the tiny issue of a panicking civilian who shouldn't have been anywhere near the clubhouse, and that wasn't exactly enhancing my mood.

I kicked the door shut after me, then carried Summer over to the bed and slid her off my shoulder and down onto it.

I reached for her hood and pulled it off so I could get a good look at her, wanting to check if she was okay. A whole lot of silky platinum-blonde hair came tumbling out and down around her shoulders, reminding me of how she used to wear it back in school, in an untidy ponytail or in a bun wound around a pen or pencil. I always used to want to tie it back properly for her since I hated untidiness as a rule, but of course I never did.

Even with her hair all down, she didn't look up. But I wasn't having that so I put a finger beneath her chin and tipped her head back so I could see her face.

Her skin was dead white, her eyes round as fucking saucers and darker than a night sky.

Jesus.

It was all coming back to me now, that month I'd spent taking her to and from school. How pissed I'd been with the Knights' then president for assigning me what had amounted to babysitting duties as a favour to the police chief. How she'd never said a word to me unless I asked her a question directly, and wouldn't meet my eyes. How much that had irritated me because, sure, I was pretty scary but I hadn't thought I was *that* scary.

She was looking at me now the same way she had back then, those big eyes glazed with fear, and it annoyed me at the same time as it made my chest feel tight. Because I hadn't wanted her to be afraid of me back then and I didn't want her to be afraid of me now. It felt…wrong somehow.

I had no idea what was up with that shit because it wasn't as if I was a nice, caring kind of guy. I was an enforcer, for fuck's sake. I made sure the brothers stuck to the club rules. And I only cared about three things—my club, my bike and making myself feel good as often as I damn well could.

Nothing else mattered.

Certainly not this scaredy-cat who'd got herself into some pretty deep shit.

But knowing all that didn't stop the tightness in my chest. And I found myself rubbing her little chin with my thumb as if I wanted to soothe her or something. 'You gonna tell me what you're doing here, baby girl?' I asked, deliberately using the name I used to call her years ago, when I'd wanted to get a rise out of her. I'd always figured that since being nice to her hadn't got her to be less scared of me, maybe getting her angry would work. 'Did Crash hurt you? Because I'm telling you right now that if he did, his name is going straight to the top of my shitlist.'

She didn't respond to me 'baby girl'-ing her. Instead she swallowed and I found myself staring at

the pulse beating in the hollow of her throat. It was
fast. Way too fucking fast.

'Tiger?' she said at long last, her voice husky and
uncertain.

Hearing her say my name like that shocked me. I
didn't know she'd even remembered it, because she'd
certainly never used it to my face.

'Yeah, you know it.' Her skin was incredibly soft
and smooth under my thumb and I couldn't seem
to stop myself from stroking her again. I'd touched
plenty of other women so there was no reason why
her skin should feel any different. But somehow it
did.

She blinked a couple more times, staring at me
as if she'd never seen me before in her entire life.
Then her gaze slowly dropped to… Holy shit. She
was looking at my mouth.

That thing inside me kicked again, harder this
time, and I felt my cock stir.

Christ, what the fuck was she doing that for?
Didn't she know what a come on it was?

As if I'd said it out loud, those big blue eyes came
back to mine again, and she must have realised what
she was doing because suddenly colour washed over
her pale skin and she jerked herself out of my grip.

'Don't,' she muttered, bending her head again and
looking at her hands twisting in her lap, the long
blonde hair in a curtain around her face.

'Okay. So you can talk.' I resisted the urge to
grab her again, settling for putting my hands in my
pockets instead. The warmth of her skin against
my fingertips lingered, which pissed me off for no

good reason. 'You wanna answer my question about Crash?'

She was silent and I thought she was going to retreat, but then she said finally, 'He didn't hurt me. He was just…insistent.'

'More than insistent. Looked like he scared the shit out of you.'

'I wasn't s-scared.'

'Yeah, and I'm the fucking Queen of England.'

She didn't say anything to that, her hands whiteknuckled in her lap.

Christ, this silence bullshit was starting to get really fucking annoying.

'What the hell are you doing here, Summer?' I demanded, coming to the end of my patience. 'And look at me when I'm talking to you.'

Finally, she lifted her head, and maybe I was imagining things, but it seemed like her eyes were less dark. I saw a small blue spark had flickered to life in them.

If it was anger, then good. That was way better than fear.

'Maybe I just wanted to hang out with some b-bikers,' she said, a defensive note in her voice.

I nearly laughed. 'Seriously? You were nearly catatonic back there, baby girl. So, no, I'm not buying you wanting to hang out with some bikers.'

That pretty mouth of hers thinned. 'I'm not a baby and I'm not a girl.'

Yeah, looked like I was annoying her, which was excellent. It also looked like she had a bit of spirit in her after all. Certainly more than she'd had when she was seventeen.

Yeah, and you like that, too.

Which I was *not* going to think about.

'I don't care who you are,' I said mildly. 'You've got five seconds to give me the truth or I'm taking you straight to Keep and you can tell him.'

Fear flashed in her eyes again, but this time that determined chin firmed. Another good sign. 'Don't do that. Please.'

'Okay, well, you'd better start doing some talking then, hadn't you?'

Her gaze flicked away from mine. 'Well…um… I… It's…uh…'

'Use your words, baby girl.'

It flicked back, another of those blue sparks flashing, the colour in her cheeks pinker. Much, *much* better. Annoying her was clearly the way to go. Which was excellent considering I was a master at annoying the shit out of people.

'Give me one good reason I should tell you.' She lifted that chin, looking down her nose at me, all haughty and shit. And fuck knows why, but my cock found that extremely hot.

'Because I asked you,' I said gently, ignoring my impatient dick.

She frowned. 'That's not a good enough reason.'

Holy shit, this woman was a problem.

'Baby girl,' I explained, trying to be patient, 'the way I see it, you have two choices. You either tell me what's going on right now. Or you tell me what's going on right now.'

Her frown deepened. 'But…those two are the same.'

I folded my arms and gave her my enforcer's smile. The one guaranteed to make a brother wish they'd never been born. 'Yeah. I know.'

CHAPTER THREE

Summer

I SAT ON Tiger's bed and stared at him, feeling something deep inside me quiver in a way that had nothing whatsoever to do with the weird panic that had overtaken me in Crash's room.

Or rather, it felt related to fear but not like I was in imminent danger of death or anything. More like when you get on a rollercoaster or a plane taking off, and everything is fast and out of control and it's freaky and scary at the same time.

Tiger had always had that effect on me. He had been exciting and scary and I just hadn't known what to do with myself around him.

I still didn't.

Him suddenly appearing in Crash's room like some kind of tattooed avenging angel, bringing all my confused teenaged feelings about him flooding back, had made me freeze. Like I just…couldn't deal with Crash and him *and* where I was and what was happening all at the same time. And then he'd picked me up and tossed me over his shoulder like I weighed nothing at all and my brain had simply shut down.

Sometimes it happened to me like that. When I got overwhelmed, I froze. As if I was afraid something worse might happen if I moved.

I hated it. Or rather, I hated myself when I got like that. Especially when it happened in front of someone so strong and in control.

Someone like Tiger.

And he was just as strong and in control now as he had been back when I was seventeen. Just as tall and muscular. Just as scary. And just as freaking hot.

He was in jeans and a blue T-shirt, that biker leather vest over the top, and he had his arms folded, giving me a glimpse of the incredible tattoos inked into the bronze skin covering the powerful muscles of his biceps and forearms.

On his right arm, a tiger prowled, long and lean and dangerous, its teeth bared. On his left, an intricate, dizzying design of interlocking circles and spirals and all sorts of other geometries. For a second I got distracted, too busy staring at it and trying to follow all the angles to remember that he'd asked me a question.

'Baby girl,' he said quietly, in that deep voice that I felt right down low in my belly, 'I'm not gonna ask again.'

Baby girl. Hadn't he heard me when I'd told him I didn't like it? How annoying. I'd hated it back when he'd been my protector, had found it incredibly patronising, but I'd been too shy to tell him to stop.

I had a bit more backbone now, though I got distracted again by the warning note in his voice.

Crap. He was going to make me tell him, wasn't he? God, what the hell was I going to do now? I didn't want him to find out what a coward I was. Or how ridiculously stupid I'd been to come down here without a plan.

No, I shouldn't have cared what he thought of me, but the fact was, I did.

He was so strong and bright and...vivid. He didn't give a shit what anyone thought of him. He did whatever the hell he wanted.

He was everything that I wasn't and that intimidated the crap out of me, and the thought of having to spill my guts to him about Dad and my generally being pathetic when it came to emotional manipulation made me feel ill.

But what choice did I have?

Well, you could try distracting him...

That was an option, of course. But how? I wasn't especially good at small talk and found talking to people in general difficult. Particularly people who intimidated me.

I bit my lip and frowned at him. My panic seemed to have receded, which was a mercy, my brain functioning again, formulating several plans, then discarding them.

Maybe I should ask him about his tattoos. Didn't guys like talking about themselves? And if I managed to get him talking, then I wouldn't have to, an added bonus.

Taking a silent breath, I pushed myself off his bed and took a couple of uncertain steps towards him.

He watched me approach, those golden eyes on mine, unblinking, and I felt fear curl up tight once again inside me. But I made myself take another step or two, getting nearer.

He was even more intimidating close up. I wasn't short, yet he towered over me, a wall of hard muscle and raw masculine power, sending my heartbeat racing into overdrive.

My mouth was dry and I felt shaky, and I had to force myself to speak. 'Your t-tattoos are amazing,' I stuttered weakly. 'Where did you get them?'

This close to him I could feel the heat of his body and smell that delicious scent I remembered from years ago. Leather and engine oil, and some kind of dark spice that made me want to bury my face in his neck and inhale.

Unlike Crash, the thought of being near Tiger didn't make me want to either cringe or pull away. No, it made me want to get even closer.

God, he made my head swim. Like he had when he'd taken my chin in his hand and rubbed it with his thumb. I'd forgotten my fear the moment he'd touched me, the very second those incredible eyes of his had met mine. And instead of feeling like I was going to freeze to death, I'd felt hot instead. Far, far too hot.

He'd been so close, his beautifully sculpted face right in front of me. And I hadn't been able to stop myself from looking at his mouth, with that full bottom lip that had fascinated me so completely at seventeen.

It still fascinated me, and, like I had back then, I'd found myself wondering what it would be like to have that mouth on mine. I'd never been kissed before so I had nothing to compare it to, only that half excited, half fearful wondering...

'Jesus Christ,' Tiger said, his dark voice rolling over me, making me feel like he'd wrapped me up in black velvet. 'I swear to God if you don't start telling me what the fuck is going on, I'm going to call the cops right now and get them to pick you up.'

His golden eyes were full of impatience and anger, and the way he was staring at me made me feel lightheaded and dizzy.

So much for distraction. It had been a lame conversation starter anyway.

I dragged my gaze away, trying to control my sudden breathlessness, not wanting want him to know how badly he affected me. I was even shocked at it myself, especially since it had been a good five years since I'd seen him.

'Okay, okay.' I turned around and went to sit on the double bed pushed up against the opposite wall.

Unlike Crash's room, Tiger's was scrupulously neat, which surprised me, though I wasn't sure why. The floor was clear of clothes, the quilt straight on the bed. Even the male toiletries and other paraphernalia on the dresser were neatly lined up. Obviously Tiger liked a tidy room, a fact I filed away like I'd filed away other salient facts I'd learned about him in the one month during which he'd guarded me. Not that there were many, since I'd been too tongue-tied to ask him any questions.

But I knew he kept a gun in the small of his back and that he had the most amazing, sexy grin that he turned on any pretty woman who came near him. I knew he rode his bike like it was part of him and that he'd taken his job of protecting me very seriously indeed. Even though he'd hated it, which he'd made very obvious.

You know there's another way to distract him. One that doesn't involve conversation.

My brain came to a screaming halt as the thought crossed my mind and my face heated.

Oh, yes, well. There was *that*. Which was all very well if I'd been some kind of practised seductress. But I wasn't. I was Summer Grant, and I'd spent most of my life trying to be invisible to as many people as possible.

I was the classic nerd. I had been at school, and the same in college. And since mostly it made people leave me alone, I was okay with it. I didn't miss parties or the desperate drama that went along with dating. I was happy with my studies, losing myself in numbers and equations, where everything was logical and followed clear rules. It was easier and way more interesting than all the usual college/teenage stuff that other people got up to.

I'd never met anyone I'd wanted enough to bear the hassle of it anyway.

Well, anyone except Tiger.

He was staring at me, that gaze of his almost flattening me with its intensity. He was leaning back against the closed door now, his arms folded across his muscular chest, the black geometries of his fascinating tattoos dark on his skin.

I felt his stare like a pressure around my throat, closing off all my air, leaving me in no doubt that he wanted an answer and he wanted it now.

Taking a breath, I got up again, a weird kind of restlessness pacing under my skin. I closed the distance between us, coming right up to where he stood. Even nearer than I had before.

His amber gaze followed me so intently it made me almost dry-mouthed with terror. I didn't quite know why. I only knew that the way he looked at me, as if he could really *see* me, made me feel vulnerable in a way I couldn't describe.

It made me want to run away and hide.

But I couldn't, not here. There was nowhere to run to and, besides, I had a feeling Tiger wouldn't let me anyway.

All I could do was keep walking until I was right up close to him, so there were only inches between us. He never took his eyes off me, not once, and again, this near to him, I felt the weird dizziness take over. His scent and his heat and his golden gaze…

'I was in Crash's room because…' I faltered but then made myself go on. 'Well…I wanted to see what being with a b-biker was like.'

Tiger stared down at me for a long moment and I could see something that looked like annoyance glinting in his gaze. Then his mouth curved in a smile that had nothing to do with amusement and he gave a soft laugh that made a shiver chase down my spine. 'Right,' he said. 'So all you want is biker cock.' He gave another laugh. 'Try again, baby girl.'

I don't know what happened then. Maybe it was just being here and running out of options. Maybe it was some leftover stupidity from me shoving Crash away. Whatever it was, his obvious disbelief made a small spark of annoyance ignite me.

It was insanity to argue with a man like Tiger, a man who radiated violence and danger, who had menace inked into his skin. Yet for some reason I opened my big fat mouth and said, 'How do you know that's not why I'm here? Biker c-cock might be exactly what I want.'

There was a stunning silence.

Tiger finally blinked and I was conscious of a weird warm feeling in amongst all that cold fear. Had I finally surprised him?

Of course it didn't last long.

He bent his head and suddenly his face was millimetres from mine, those amber eyes boring into me, that beautiful mouth so close. 'If biker cock is really what you want, then what are you waiting for? I'm a biker and I have a cock. Get down on your knees and suck it.'

The shock of the words and his abrupt nearness froze me in place. But not like before, in Crash's room. I wasn't rigid with fear this time, because I could read in his gaze that he wasn't serious. This was a dare. He used to do that in the month when he'd been my protector, teasing me to get a rise out of me. I'd always been too afraid to respond to him then but now…

I don't know what came over me. A sudden rush of anger filled me, along with a determination to show him that I wasn't the scared 'baby girl' he seemed to think I was.

Forgetting my fear, I gave him one furious look. Then I dropped to my knees in front of him.

CHAPTER FOUR

Tiger

NOTHING SURPRISED ME much any more. But little Summer Grant dropping to her knees right in front of me, ready to prove she was desperate to suck my cock?

Yeah, not gonna lie, that surprised the hell out of me.

Telling her to get on her knees was supposed to have made her back off, not actually do what I said.

I didn't move, looking down at her as she knelt in front of me. Of course I knew that she didn't actually want to do this—I hadn't missed that blue spark that had lit in her eyes just before she did what I told her to do.

She was calling my bluff the way I'd called hers.

And, fuck, she might just have won this round, because, Christ, I couldn't actually let her suck me off. Not given how terrified she'd been not fifteen minutes earlier in Crash's room. And not when she was only doing this because it was clear she didn't want to tell me what she was *actually* doing in the clubhouse.

Unfortunately, though, my goddamn cock didn't seem to understand that.

There was something about the way she knelt in front of me, with her chin lifted, her eyes on mine. And I could see that spark of anger dancing in them. Yeah, she definitely wasn't the scaredy-cat she appeared to be.

In fact, if I wasn't much mistaken, she was giving me a challenge to answer the one I'd just given her.

Not many brothers took me on these days, let alone one little girl. That took guts.

And it made me hard.

Made me want to reach down and bury my fingers in all that silky blonde hair, hold on to her as she took my dick, as she worked her mouth on me, taking me deep.

Made me want to know how far I could push her, how far I could go. Did that little spark of hers mean she was steel all the way through, or would she shatter if I put pressure on her?

I suspected I knew already, though. I suspected she was steel. It was always the quiet ones you had to watch out for, those were the ones with claws.

Christ, that mouth of hers was to die for. Perfectly shaped and a little red from where she'd been gnawing on it. I could imagine those lips wrapped around my cock, could imagine tasting them as well. Maybe biting on them to see if they were as soft as they looked.

But, shit, I had to get a handle on myself. I couldn't

goad her into blowing me. It wasn't what she was here for, no matter that she was insisting otherwise. And apart from anything else, I wasn't in the mood to be giving dick-sucking advice to virgins.

Yeah, sure. You're not in the mood. Like hell.

Ignoring my cock thoughts, I didn't move, only shook my head. 'I'm glad you're keen, baby, but no. We're not doing that.'

Those big blue eyes widened in what I thought was genuine surprise—for some reason it made me glad I could surprise her the way she'd surprised me—and that pouty mouth opened. 'Oh, but I thought you said—'

'I know what I said.' I cut her off. 'I fucking changed my mind. Now, go sit back on that bed like a good girl.'

Again that blue spark jumped, like she was pissed or maybe disappointed, which I didn't mind at all, not one bit, then she got to her feet and went slowly back over to the bed once more. She sat down and looked at her hands again, resolutely avoiding my gaze, her shoulders slumping.

Okay, so it was definitely disappointment. But… why? She hadn't *really* wanted to suck my dick, had she? Not after she'd been so goddamn terrified.

Why are you thinking about this shit? Why the fuck does it matter?

Both very good questions and ones I didn't have the answers to.

Just like I *still* didn't know why the hell she was here.

I was about to give her the hard word yet a-fucking-*gain*, when someone's fist connected loudly on the door at my back. 'Tiger.' It was Keep, sounding pissed. 'I need to talk to you. Open the fucking door.'

At the sound of Keep's voice, Summer's chin came up, her gaze getting wide and dark, frightened again.

Interesting. So given how she hadn't wanted me to talk to Keep earlier and her reaction to the sound of his voice now, it was obvious that she really didn't want him to know she was here. Which kind of made sense. She probably knew he'd bundle her up and ship her out the moment he discovered her.

Keep hammered on the door again, louder this time, and Summer's gaze came to mine, the desperation in it loud and clear. She *really* didn't want me to give her away.

It was crazy. The first thing I should have done was open the door and let my president inside, show him who was hiding out in my room. Because the club came first and always had done, and she represented trouble for it, no doubt about that.

Yet for some reason, that look in her eyes made my chest tighten yet again. Been a long, long time since someone had looked at me like that. Not since my little brother had disappeared along with my mom. Looking at me as if I could help them. As if I could save them.

So when I opened my mouth, it wasn't 'Sure, Keep, come in' that came out. It was 'Gimme a minute, Prez. I'm kind of busy.'

Summer let out a small, sharp breath, like she'd been holding it.

Then Keep said very distinctly, 'Open the fucking door. I don't care who you've got in there.'

Shit.

I couldn't say no to my president and Summer must have known that, because her face went white, and she went very still. And she kept her gaze on mine, silently pleading.

So I made a snap decision.

Pushing myself away from the door, I strode over to the bed and jerked the quilt out from under her. 'Get in,' I ordered.

She blinked rapidly. 'W-what?'

'You want me to hide you? Then get the fuck in my bed.'

She hesitated only a second, kicking off her stilettos before crawling into my bed and drawing the covers up to her chin. While she did that, I shrugged off my cut and slung it over the end of the bed, then pulled my T-shirt off.

'Tiger!' Keep was sounding really pissed now. 'For fuck's sake.'

Summer was watching me with those big eyes getting rounder as I pulled the quilt from her fingers. 'If you want this to work,' I said shortly, quietly, 'then don't argue and follow my lead, okay?'

She didn't speak, only nodded.

So I got into bed with her, positioning myself over the top of her, covering her with my body. Then I pulled the quilt over us.

And not before time.

The door slammed open and there was Keep, standing in the doorway, one of the meanest mother-fuckers in the whole MC.

'Sorry, Prez,' I said lazily, looking around at him. 'I should have said. The door's open.'

He gave me that long, hard president's stare, taking in the fact that I was in bed and that there was very obviously a woman with me. My elbows were on the pillows on either side of Summer's head, my upper arms shielding her. Her hair was all over my pillow and she'd turned her face away. There was no way Keep would know who she was, as long as I didn't move.

'Thought you would have been out in the corridor,' he said flatly. 'You're such a fucking exhibitionist.'

Summer was trembling a little, her body warm and soft beneath mine, the flower scent of hers wrapping around me like I'd stumbled into a fucking garden. Her legs were spread and I could feel the intense heat of her pussy pressing against the zipper of my jeans, soaking into the denim.

This wasn't a mistake. At all.

Christ, what the hell else was I supposed to do? There'd been nowhere else for her to hide. Pretending she was some chick I'd brought in to fuck had been the only option.

I forced myself to ignore the feel of her beneath me and said, 'Yeah, well, today I thought I'd be really kinky and try for some privacy.' I shifted my hips, like I was halfway up inside her already and wanted to keep going. 'Speaking of, you got something serious to ask me? 'Cause as you can see, there's something else I'd much rather be doing.'

Keep grunted, his blue eyes cold. 'Got word that Campbell Grant's daughter has gone missing and he wanted me to keep an eye out for her.'

I could feel Summer go rigid under me and I didn't need to see her face to know that the thought of being discovered scared her. Of course it made me want to know why, because although I didn't know much about the police chief, I knew plenty about his asshole son, Summer's brother. Justin Grant was the ex of Cat Livingston, my friend Smoke's old lady. He'd been violent towards her and some shit had gone down that had included Smoke teaching the prick a lesson.

I didn't like the thought of Summer being exposed to that kind of crap, and if the son had been like that, what about the father? Sure, I'd never known what it was like to have a dad since I'd grown up without one, but I knew what had happened with Smoke's old man and Smoke had told me about Cat's.

Seemed like fathers in general were assholes.

'Yeah, I haven't seen her.' I looked down at the woman lying very still under me. She had her face still turned away, her hair covering her cheek.

Was it her father she was scared of? Was that why she'd come down here? But why here? There were plenty of other less dangerous places to hide than a biker clubhouse. What about friends? Other family?

'Maybe you should start looking,' Keep said. 'Once you've finished, obviously.'

I didn't look at my president, as I was too busy

frowning down at Summer. 'Yeah, okay. Might take a while, though.'

'This is more important than your dick, Tiger,' Keep growled. 'The chief's still pissed about that fucker Justin so we've got some ground to make up. Be good if one of the Knights could locate her and bring her in. If she hasn't simply run away, of course.'

Summer did that freezing-in-place thing again. And I wanted to grip her chin and turn her head to face me, look into her eyes to make sure she was okay. But I didn't want to risk Keep seeing her, so all I said was 'Gotcha, Prez. I'll finish up here and then I'm on it.' Quite literally in fact, but he wasn't to know that.

Keep didn't say another word, but I heard the door slam shut and then silence.

Summer remained still and that was actually starting to become something of a problem. Because my brain kept on wanting to concentrate on that heat between her legs and it was starting to get me hard.

No, scratch 'starting to.' I'd been hard even before getting into bed with her.

Which makes getting into bed with her a pretty fucking dumb idea, don't you think? Especially when you shouldn't even be touching her.

Yeah, okay, maybe it was. But I wasn't a goddamn teenage boy. I was the one in control, not my fucking cock. Which meant I should have been throwing back the quilt and getting off her, putting some distance between us.

Yet I didn't move. I stayed right where I was. I

was bracing myself on my elbows so I wasn't actually lying on her, but her tits were almost brushing my chest. I couldn't see much of them since she was wearing a loose hoodie, but they seemed high and rounded, a nice handful.

And now you're staring at her tits? What the fuck is wrong with you?

It was an excellent point and yet I still couldn't seem to make myself get off her. And what was more, I was beginning to think that this was actually a great time to make her tell me what the hell she was doing here.

'Summer,' I said quietly. 'He's gone.'

A quiver ran the entire length of her body. I could damn well feel it. Then, slowly, she turned her head, giving me a quick glance from beneath her lashes, like she was afraid to look at me. But there was a flush of pink on her cheekbones, a pretty good indication to me that she wasn't scared. Or at least not as scared as she had been.

Fuck, she was so hot, though. That little pussy of hers felt like a fire burning through my zipper and if I wasn't much mistaken—and I seldom was—I thought I'd caught a hint of musk threading through her sweet, flowery scent.

Whatever you're thinking, it's not a good idea, dumb fuck.

Of course it wasn't a good idea. It was a fucking terrible idea. Yet I still wasn't moving, staying there braced on my elbows with my cock pressed hard between her legs.

She made a restless movement and her hands

came up, long, pale fingers pressing against my chest. Then, like my body was a stove she'd accidentally burned herself on, she jerked them away again. 'T-Tiger...' she muttered thickly, still avoiding my gaze. 'I th-think you should...uh...move.'

I don't know what it was about hearing my name in her mouth. Plenty of women called me by it and yet I'd never once felt it go straight to my cock the way it did right now. Maybe it was her voice, all soft and husky and uncertain, and that goddamn stutter on the *T*. Like she was afraid to say it.

The club girls didn't say my name like that. They didn't avoid my gaze, jerk their hands away from my bare skin and blush like a fucking rose. And when they did look at me, it wasn't with fear or excitement or any shit like that. Sure, they wanted me, but they didn't much care who got them off. One cock was as good as another as far as they were concerned.

It had never bothered me before.

It had never bothered me before that one cock was as good as another for them. As long as everyone came, I was fine with it. And as for civilians, well, I didn't mess around with them, because I wasn't up for anything more complicated than fucking.

But Summer, she was lying there all pink and flushed, and avoiding my gaze. And it wasn't because she didn't want me. Because if she hadn't, she'd be shoving me like she'd shoved Crash, and there was definitely no shoving going on.

Yeah, I knew when a woman was into me and this little girl was into me. Not Crash. Not some other brother. *Me*.

And I didn't just like that.

I fucking loved it.

'Uh-huh,' I murmured, staying right where I was, because I was an asshole. 'And how exactly do you want me to move, baby girl?'

CHAPTER FIVE

Summer

I COULDN'T THINK. I could barely even breathe.

I'd always been proud of my brain since it was about the only thing about me that made me special. But right now, with Tiger lying right on top of me, it was like I'd lost several thousand brain cells and the stupid thing was refusing to work.

He was just so…*hot*. And…*big*. And he was everywhere, his bare chest right in front of me, his wide shoulders blocking out the rest of the room, his long, lean, muscular body pressed the whole length of mine.

And his gaze looking down at me, drowning me in gold.

I didn't know what to do with my hands. I didn't know what to do with my entire *self*.

It had happened so fast. One minute I was feeling half disappointed, half relieved that he'd pulled me up off my knees, and maybe a little angry at myself, too, since I hadn't managed to distract him, which meant that now he was going to make me tell him my real reason for being here. Then the next minute there had been a knocking at the door and I'd heard Keep's voice.

I'd thought Tiger would turn me in.

But he hadn't. He'd come across to the bed and told me to get in, and since I hadn't exactly had a lot of choice, I'd kicked off my shoes and done so. The next thing I knew, he'd ripped off his T-shirt and had climbed in, too, lying on top of me, bracing himself on his elbows so he wasn't resting his whole weight on me.

I'd never been in bed with anyone before, let alone the man who'd been lurking in my head ever since I was seventeen. The man who was now half-naked, his hard, sculpted chest and powerful shoulders on show. And somehow it didn't matter that he wasn't resting entirely on me, I felt flattened by him anyway. By the sheer intensity of his physical presence. By his closeness. By the heat of his body and the scent of his bare skin.

My brain shut down then, simply unable to function with Tiger being so near. And then Keep was in the room and finally I realised why Tiger had told me to get into bed and why he was lying on top of me.

He was hiding me from Keep.

The thought was brief and bright and then it disappeared, and I forgot completely that Keep was even in the room. Because somehow my skirt had got rucked up around my waist, my bare thighs brushing against the denim of Tiger's jeans. His hips were resting between my legs, forcing them apart, and there was something big and thick and hard pressing against the front of my panties.

And once I'd become conscious of that, I couldn't concentrate on anything else. There was something about the pressure of him right *there* that made me go hot all over. That made my thighs tremble and my breathing catch. I tried to hold myself rigid, to pull away from where he was touching me, but it was impossible.

He was everywhere. His heat and his dark, spicy scent and all that smooth tanned skin right in front of me. The fascinating tattoo of all the spirals and circles that was on his upper arm went up and over his shoulder, too, spreading halfway across his broad chest. I had to turn my head away to stop from staring at it, my fingers itching to touch it.

But not looking at him didn't do anything to stop the aching awareness of him. The feeling of his long, hot body over mine, pressing down on me, overwhelming me.

He was still overwhelming me.

Keep had gone, yet Tiger was still lying on top of me, braced on his elbows on either side of my head, looking down at me. I could feel myself getting hotter and hotter, and I didn't want to meet his gaze. I didn't want him to see what he was doing to me, how completely overcome I was about this whole situation.

God, my fingertips were tingling from where I'd made the mistake of touching his chest just before—his skin had been so hot I felt like he'd scorched me—so I closed them into fists, not sure where to put them except awkwardly down at my sides.

I knew he'd asked me a question and I was struggling to remember what it was, acutely conscious of the intense heat between my legs where his zipper was pressing against me, making me feel restless and achy and desperate.

He'd said something about moving, right?

'I don't want you to move.' I tried not to look up into his unblinking amber gaze. 'I just want you to get off me.'

'Uh-huh.' His voice sounded lazy, a deep rumble I felt echo down the length of my body. 'Okay, just gimme a second. I'm getting all caught up in the sheet.'

Then he shifted his hips.

It was only a slight movement, but somehow it nudged the hard ridge of his zipper over my clit, sending a lightning strike of sensation firing through me, lighting up every single nerve ending I had.

I tensed, gasping in shock at the unexpectedness of it.

Tiger stilled. 'You okay?' he asked in that same soft, lazy rumble, sounding completely unconcerned.

I couldn't look at him, little pulses of sensation sparking everywhere and my heartbeat—already fast—starting to get frantic.

I might have been a virgin, but I wasn't completely ignorant. I mean, I had a vibrator and I knew how to use it, so this feeling wasn't exactly new. Except that it wasn't anything like the calm, gentle pleasure I gave myself on occasion. This sensation was brighter, sharper, more vivid. Electric.

And one I had no control over whatsoever.

'I…uh…' I tried to catch my breath, tried to hide how much that slight movement of his had affected me. 'Y-yes. I just…need you to get off me.' Now. Please, God, right now.

'Impatient, huh? Where's the fire?' He shifted again, another roll of his hips over that achingly sensitive spot between my thighs, sending another burst of that intense, brilliant sensation exploding through me.

I jerked, instinctively looking up at him, as if his gaze was a magnet and I couldn't resist the pull.

Gold slammed into me. Bright, flaming gold. Burning me, *seeing* me. A forest fire and there was nowhere for me to run, nowhere for me to hide.

I trembled, scared for reasons I couldn't have described. 'T-Tiger…'

'Yeah, I know.' His hands moved, cupping either side of my jaw, the touch of his palms against my skin making me tremble harder. 'I like the way you say my name. Thought you didn't remember it.'

I blinked, trying to breathe. Trying to concentrate on what he was saying and not on the ache that was building between my thighs, right where he was pressing down. But it was so difficult. 'I…I… just need…'

'Need what, hmm?' He rolled his hips yet again, another slow, delicious grind that pressed against my clit, making me jerk and shiver like he'd given me an electric shock. 'You need more of this, maybe?'

I could feel myself break out into a sweat. My thighs were trembling and I wanted to lift my hips against that tantalising pressure, to chase that incredible friction. But enough of my brain was operating to know that this was a really bad idea. Because letting *anyone* know how you felt was always a bad idea, especially when you were as lousy at hiding your feelings as I was. Especially when you were somehow in bed with a dangerous biker who'd been in your head for years. Who lingered there like a fascinating equation you could never quite work out the solution to.

'N-no.' I tried to get my voice working, the word coming out thick and husky and ragged. 'I want to… get out…'

'Really?' He shifted, another subtle movement of his hips rubbing against me, that ridge somehow bigger and harder than it had been before. I groaned, unable to help myself, pleasure beginning to wrap itself around me.

'Are you sure you want to get out?' His thumbs moved over my jaw, stroking my skin, adding more fuel to the fire burning hotter and hotter. 'Seems to me like what you want is more of this.' And he moved again as if to illustrate the point, nearly making my eyes roll back in my head.

I'd begun to pant, my pulse thudding so loud it was a wonder he couldn't hear it, too. I could barely take in what he was saying to me. All I was aware of was the gold in his eyes and the sweet, sharp pleasure he was giving me.

He began to set up a rhythm, making the whole world shudder. Making my skin feel too tight and like I couldn't get enough air. Like I was hot. Too hot.

'What are you doing?' I gasped rather belatedly, raising my fists to push at him, only remembering at the last moment what a bad idea that was. 'I can't… This isn't…'

'It's okay, baby girl,' he said in that dark rumble, his thumbs moving in a gentle back and forth along my jawline. The touch was almost tender in comparison to the way he was moving against me, the pleasure as he rolled over my clit almost vicious, making me moan helplessly. 'Just making you feel good.'

And it *was* good. It was *so* good.

'W-why?' I stammered, trying not to let myself get swept away by what he was doing to me. Trying not to give in to the urges that my body was sending me, to spread my legs wider, lift my hips, rub against him, grab some of that insane, delicious friction that was driving me crazy.

'Why?' Tiger echoed, seeming almost surprised by the question. 'Why the fuck not?' He slowed the rhythm a little, making it hard, more relentless, sending a shower of white-hot sparks cascading through me. 'You're sweet and you're sexy. And your little pussy's as hot as fuck.' His gaze intensified, his thumb brushing along my lower lip. 'Also, I don't like it when little girls who don't know what they're doing try and use blow jobs to distract me. Makes me want to give them a taste of their own medicine.'

I couldn't process that. I couldn't even breathe. The pleasure he was giving me was crushing me completely. 'I can't tell you,' I whispered, barely aware of what I was saying. 'I c-can't… I don't want to…'

'Hey, hey. Stop that.' His voice was dark and

rough, and felt like a caress over my bare skin. 'All I want you to think about is what I'm doing right now, hmm?'

Again he moved, another slow grind right against my achingly sensitive clit, and this time I couldn't stop my hips from lifting and my back from arching, pressing myself harder against him.

'Oh, yeah,' he whispered roughly. 'That's it. Rub that little pussy against my dick, baby. Get yourself off.'

I should have hated the dirty words. They should have made me uncomfortable the way they had when Crash had said them. But they didn't. Somehow, spoken in Tiger's rough voice, they only made everything ten thousand times hotter.

His movements got faster, and I was moving with him, entirely by instinct. The pleasure rolling through me was making me pant, my face so hot it was like my skin was on fire.

'You're all wet.' The relentless grind of Tiger's hips was an irresistible rhythm I had no hope of fighting. 'I can feel you soaking my jeans. You like this, don't you? Feels good, right?'

'Y-yes.' I couldn't stop the word from slipping out and as soon as I said it, the brilliant gold of his eyes flared even hotter.

'How good, baby? Tell me how I'm making you feel right now.'

It was an order and I found myself obeying helplessly. 'S-so good,' I gasped. 'I can't... It's too much...'

His beautiful mouth curved in a slow, deeply sexy

smile, as if he liked what I'd said. 'Oh, it's not too much. In fact, I'd say it's not nearly enough.'

Then he slowed his movement right down, each shift of his hips lazy and relentless, the pressure on my clit becoming almost unbearable.

I groaned, starting to shake and unable to stop.

'You ever had a guy do this to you before?' Tiger's gaze was inescapable as it searched mine. 'You ever had anyone make you come?'

I didn't want to admit it, didn't want him to know exactly how inexperienced I was. But there was no way I could pretend I did this kind of thing all the time. There was no way I could pretend anything at all right now.

So all I did was stare back at him, letting him read the truth plastered all over my face.

His smile got hotter, as if this was the best thing he'd heard all day. 'You didn't come down here for Crash, did you? You came down here for me.'

There was something in the way he said the last sentence that I knew I should pay attention to. But the sensation between my thighs was getting too much to bear and all I could think was, yes, I *had* come down here for Tiger.

He's the one you run to when you want to be safe.

The thought flashed through my brain, bright as a comet, then disappeared, crushed by the weight of the pleasure that was building inside me.

It was too intense, too fast, and for some reason it scared me.

'Tiger,' I whispered yet again, abruptly frantic. 'I don't know... I can't...'

'Hold on to me.'

It was another order and I obeyed without thought, too, my hands clutching on the heavy muscle of his shoulders. I felt him tense as I touched him, the heat of his skin like a hot coal against my fingertips. I didn't jerk away this time, my nails digging in. He was solid, grounding me, an anchor holding me down as the storm building inside me began to shake me apart.

I said his name again, sweat breaking out all over my body as the dark pleasure he was giving me began to escape my grip.

No, this was *nothing* like my vibrator, where I could control the pleasure I gave myself. Where I could stop if it got to be too much or make it harder if it wasn't enough. This was out of my control completely.

The sensation was terrifying, like I was on the back of a motorcycle I had no idea how to ride, and it was going faster and faster. And I couldn't find the brake to slow it down or the keys to turn the engine off.

I had no choice but to hold on and pray to God I didn't fall off.

My nails dug harder into his shoulders as everything began to spiral out of control. I didn't know what was going to happen when this pressure released and I was afraid I was going to shatter or break apart. That I was going to be in pieces and no one was going to be able to put me back together again.

He must have known what was happening to me,

must have read my fear. Because his long, muscular body settled over mine, his weight pressing me down against the mattress, surrounding me. Holding me. And he lowered his head, so his face was only inches away. 'Look at me, baby girl,' he murmured, those gold eyes of his taking up my whole world. 'And hold on tight. I've got you.'

So I did. I held on and I looked at him.

And when the pressure began to release and the orgasm exploded through me, and I opened my mouth to scream, his lips were on mine.

And all I could see was gold.

CHAPTER SIX

Tiger

I KISSED HER. Not because I wanted to keep her quiet—I loved making women scream—but I just couldn't keep myself from tasting her.

Just one kiss, that was all I was going to let myself have, which, considering the fact that her little pussy was creaming all over my jeans, was the epitome of fucking restraint.

She screamed into my mouth as she came, her body tensing and arching up into mine, her nails digging into my skin. I'd meant to simply give myself a taste, but she was so sweet, like a hit of pure sugar, and I was kissing her harder before I even realised what I was doing. Her mouth was so fucking hot, and she was shuddering under me, and I couldn't seem to stop myself, sliding my hands beneath her head and cradling it as I slid my tongue between her lips.

I'd never been particularly interested in kissing. Seemed a pointless waste of time when orgasms could be happening instead, yet I found I couldn't stop kissing Summer all the same.

There was a flavour to her, one I couldn't quite put my finger on, that was erotic as hell, and was making my cock ache even more. I didn't know what the fuck it was, whether it had something to do with the fact that she was coming against me, or whether it was because she'd never had anyone do this to her before.

Yeah, okay. It *was* because she'd never had anyone do this to her before and I was the first—I'd read that particular truth in her face. Which shouldn't have turned me on, because I didn't get possessive or territorial with chicks, but it just fucking did.

No one had made her come before. And now I was kissing her, I was certain no one had done that to her before either, because although she was trying to kiss me back, she was all hesitant, like she didn't know how.

There was no reason it should have got me hard, especially when virgins weren't exactly my style. Yet I was hard. So *fucking* hard.

I wanted to rip her panties off and bury my aching cock deep in the hot pussy that was currently soaking my jeans, and fuck us both into the middle of next week.

But I wasn't going to.

She was trembling underneath me and the small, hesitant movements of her mouth beneath mine were a reminder—as if I needed one—of her complete inexperience. Which made me pretty much the worst guy on the planet for her.

I'd done everything there was to do with a woman and it took a lot to get me off these days. Dirty as fuck tended to do it and there was no way I was going to do dirty as fuck with pretty little Summer Grant, the police chief's virgin daughter.

Apparently, you don't have any objections to messing around with her, though.

I wanted to ignore the thought, to push it completely out of my head and keep on kissing the hell out of her. But it was enough of a kick in the balls to actually stop what I was doing and lift my mouth from hers.

She was staring straight up at me, the dense blue of her eyes nearly hypnotising. As was the look in them. Straight out shocked and confused, yet with an edge of what looked like wonder. Like I was the most incredible thing she'd ever seen.

It made something shift and tighten in my chest. Something uncomfortable.

Shit, no one looked at me like that any more. My little brother once had, and my mom on the nights when her clients had got rough and I'd had to intervene. But no one else. I was just another cock for the club girls, and as for the brothers, well, I was an enforcer who made them toe the line, which some of them didn't appreciate.

Irritated, I shoved the feeling away, trying to ignore it like I was trying to ignore the pain in my dick. Because apart from any of that, she was a goddamn civilian and I didn't involve myself with civilians. Not to mention the fact that she was Campbell Grant's fucking daughter, which was a whole other load of complications that neither the club nor I needed right now.

Oh, yeah, plus I *still* didn't know why she was here.

She came here for you, right?

Christ, why had I said that? I didn't actually *want* her to have come down here for me, not when I hadn't thought about her in years. Clearly a case of my dick doing my thinking for me.

'Now we've got that out of the way,' I said, my voice a lot huskier than I would have liked, 'I think it's time for you to tell me why you didn't want Keep knowing you were here.'

Her lashes came down, veiling her gaze, and her hands pushed ineffectually at my shoulders. 'Could you…give me some room?'

'No.' I made the word hard. 'No one's going anywhere until you give me the truth.' Even if my blue balls killed me.

Her cheeks were very flushed and her mouth was very red, and the heat of her pussy against my crotch was driving me fucking nuts. But I didn't move. 'Ten seconds, baby girl. Or else I call Keep right back in here.'

She let out a breath. 'I'm trying to get away from my dad,' she said at last. 'I just…wanted to go somewhere he couldn't find me.'

I gave her an incredulous look. 'What? So you thought a biker clubhouse was the perfect place? Seriously?'

This time her lashes rose and I got a hit of that little spark I'd seen in her eyes earlier, a flash of temper. 'It's the only place I could think of. The only place he'd never expect me to go, not with Keep being his friend. Also…he wouldn't think I'd be brave enough so…' She trailed off, looking away again.

Okay, so she *was* here to hide out.

Tension wound through me, and this time it didn't have anything to do with the feel of her body under mine. 'Why are you hiding from him?' I couldn't quite keep the edge out of my voice. 'He knocking you around?'

She gave me another quick, sharp glance, and I could see the fear in it this time. 'No.'

'Summer,' I said warningly.

'It's true. He hasn't.' She gave another shove at my shoulders. 'Tiger, please.'

I relented this time, both to give my fucking cock a rest and to give her some space, rolling off her and onto my side, propping my head on my elbow. My back was to the door—just in case I had any more surprise visitors—while she lay between me and the wall. It wasn't exactly what she wanted, but it was all I was prepared to give her.

This time I wasn't fucking around. I wanted answers. Because if Campbell fucking Grant was as violent as his son, I wasn't going to be very happy.

I hated men who beat on people weaker or smaller than themselves. I'd watched it happen with my mom, when I had been too small to help her, and I'd hated it then, not being able to do a thing except watch her cry.

I'd hated it even when I was bigger, when I could give those assholes a taste of their own medicine, making them cry the way they had my mom.

And I hated it now, looking at Summer. The police chief was a big man, and even though Summer was tall, she was slender. If he wanted to hurt her, he could.

The thought made me furious.

'I know your brother,' I said flatly. 'I know all about his little anger management problem. Is your dad the same? Because if he is…' I didn't finish the sentence. I didn't need to. Too bad if the asshole was a cop. He'd get what was coming to him, I'd make sure of that myself.

'Dad doesn't hit me, no.' She sat up, pulling down the hoodie she had on, then reaching down under the quilt, presumably to pull down her miniskirt.

I stared at her, watching her face and the movements she made. Her hair was a mess of white blonde all over her shoulders, and it looked pretty against the pink of her skin. She was still flushed from the orgasm I'd given her, which was incredibly fucking satisfying, even though it shouldn't have been. I could still feel her heat against my zipper and I wanted to put my hand down to feel the denim, to see if it was as wet as I suspected it was.

But finding out what she was doing here was more important than that so I stayed where I was, looking at her.

'So why are you hiding then?' I asked. 'If he's not going to hit you, then what's he going to do?'

She gave another sigh, then she bent her knees and leaned forward, wrapping her arms around her legs. 'It's a long story.'

'Baby, I've got nothing but time.'

The look in her eyes was serious. 'No, you don't. You're supposed to be out looking for me, remember? Wasn't that what Keep told you?'

'That can wait.' At least it could until she'd told

me why she was hiding. Then, depending on her reasons, I'd decide what to do about it.

'Okay,' she said, clearly reluctant. 'I graduated from college a couple of weeks ago, and just before I left, I got a really cool job offer from a tech company in Silicon Valley.'

'Oh, yeah?' After my bodyguard stint with her had ended, I'd lost track of what had happened to her, but I'd always known vaguely that she was smart, so hearing she'd gone to college wasn't a big surprise. 'Congrats.'

She flushed, as if embarrassed, which was weird. Fuck, if I'd been smart enough to go to college, I'd have been so goddamn full of myself, you wouldn't have been able to fit me and my ego in the same fucking room.

'Thanks,' she said. 'I mean, it's exciting, and I really want to go…'

'I can hear the but.'

'Yeah.' Her shoulders hunched. 'I thought Dad would be pleased about the job thing. Actually, no, I knew he *wouldn't* be pleased about the job thing, but I thought I could talk him round. Except when I told him, he wasn't happy.'

I frowned at her, not quite sure what the problem was. 'So your dad wasn't happy about you leaving. So what?'

She shook her head, the blue spark in her eyes back again. 'You don't understand. He doesn't want me to go. He wants me to stay here with him.'

Yeah, and I still didn't see the problem. 'And? Tell him to fuck off. He can't stop you.'

She glanced away, looking down at the quilt covering her knees, and shook her head slowly. 'It's not that simple.'

'Sure it is. Three words. *Fuck. Off. Dad.* Then you go. End of story.'

But she kept on shaking her head. 'It's not. I can't… say that to him. I don't…' She stopped and looked at me again. 'I can't explain it to you. It's not something you'd ever understand.'

I didn't like being dismissed. Didn't like it one fucking bit. And I especially didn't like the part about how I 'wouldn't understand.' I shouldn't have let it get to me, but for some reason, coming from her, it did.

'Ah,' I said. 'Right. So the dumb-fuck biker won't know what you're talking about, is that it?'

Her eyes widened in surprise. 'Uh, no. That's not what I meant at all.'

'Then what did you mean?'

Her colour deepened. 'I only meant that you're…' She gestured at me, as if that would explain everything. 'Well, you're tall and…strong. And you're dangerous. And you don't take crap from anyone. And I'm…not any of those things.'

Nope, still didn't know what the fuck she was talking about. 'Baby, you're gonna have to get clear about what the hell is going on real quick. Because none of this is making any sense.'

Frustration crossed her face. 'Dad manipulates things, okay? He manipulates me. And I don't want to be around him right now, because I'm afraid he'll make me change my mind and I'll end up not going to Silicon Valley after all.'

That sounded weird. But clearly it was an issue for her. She wouldn't have come down to the clubhouse in the middle of a party if it hadn't been.

'Listen,' I said, trying for gentle. 'No one can make you do anything you don't want to do. You know that, right?'

That chin of hers jutted. 'Easy for you to say. Like I told you, you're strong.'

Christ, did she really think she wasn't strong? What the fuck was that sparky attitude she kept giving me if it wasn't strength? 'And what? You're not? Bullshit to that. Anyway, being strong starts with knowing what you want and fucking taking it, not running away and cowering in a corner pretending no one can see you.'

Something flashed in her gaze again. 'I'm not running away. I just don't want to be anywhere near him for a couple of days. And anyway, I *am* taking what I want. I'm flying to California and taking that damn job.'

'Sure you are. But you're so worried your father will make you change your mind that you had to run to a biker clubhouse to hide.' Perhaps I shouldn't have said it but, shit, it was the truth.

But she didn't like that, anger lighting in her eyes. 'All that's beside the point. Are you going to hide me or not? Because if you don't, I'll find someone else who will.'

'Right, so you're going to go wandering out into the orgy currently happening in the hallway, looking for a brother to hide you?' I stared at her, not bothering to mask my scorn because—seriously?—she actually thought she could do that with no consequences whatsoever? 'Hate to say it, but if they don't take you to Keep straight away, they'll make you join in. And they're all drunk and they're all assholes. All of 'em. They'll eat you alive and I do mean that literally.'

Fear flickered across her face—she was so easy to read it wasn't funny—but that chin of hers was still stubborn. 'You'll have to hide me then.'

I nearly laughed. 'You don't get to tell me what to do, baby girl.'

'Please, Tiger.' Those big blue eyes held mine, determination and temper glowing in her gaze. 'I'll… I'll give you a blow job if you do.'

Fuck, as if I needed a reminder that my dick was still hard. 'Haven't we had this conversation already? I think I remember telling you no.'

'Please. It's only for a few days.'

'You're seriously asking me to risk my rep and my club's, not to mention my relationship with my president, just so you can hide out from your dad?' Christ, now that I'd said it aloud, the whole thing sounded insane. What the fuck was she even still doing here? I should have given her up to Keep the moment he'd come into my room and asked me to find her.

Summer swallowed and I found myself watching the movement of her lovely throat. 'What can I give you then?'

I should have said that there was nothing she could give me. Because hadn't I already decided that getting any more involved in this was a mistake? She spelled nothing but trouble for me and the club, and I'd be a fucking idiot not to get rid of her. Like, right now.

But apparently I *was* a fucking idiot, because I didn't say 'nothing.' Instead, I said, 'I don't know, baby girl. What you got?'

She squared her shoulders and looked me in the eye without a flicker. 'Me,' she said. 'I got me. You hide me, Tiger, and I'll let you do whatever you want to me.'

CHAPTER SEVEN

Summer

TIGER DIDN'T SAY anything immediately. He simply lay there on his side, his long, lean body stretched out down the entire length of the bed, his head propped on his hand, his amber gaze pinning me where I sat.

I could hear my heartbeat thumping loudly in my head and again I could feel that irritating cold current of fear. But I was determined. Sure, he might say all those things about taking what you want and not hiding, but it was fine for him. He was a man. He was strong, he took what he wanted, and most of all, he didn't care what anyone thought of him.

But that was my problem. I *did* care. I cared way too much. Yes, my dad was difficult and living with him was like living in a house made of glass. You had to be really careful because if you walked too heavily, the floor might crack and shatter under your feet, cutting you to pieces.

I'd learned to walk softly over the years, to not make a fuss. To be invisible when his mood was bad, which since Mom had left was pretty much all the time. But he was all I had. There was my older brother, Justin, but Justin had a violent temper like Dad and often flew into terrible rages. He used to pick on me a lot when I was younger, but then I got the hang of being invisible and so he left me alone.

After a while, they both did. But only because I didn't rock the boat or cause a fuss. Telling Dad I would be leaving for Silicon Valley whether he liked it or not was definitely causing a fuss, and I was afraid of what he might do. Of what he might say. He'd be angry and I hated his anger. I always had. It made me feel small and weak and powerless.

But what was the use explaining that to Tiger? Of hoping he'd understand? He wasn't a guy who let anyone's anger bother him. He just didn't give a shit. And since I couldn't explain it to him in a way he'd get and hope he'd help out of the goodness of his heart, I was left with only offering myself in return.

I knew it wasn't much, but it was all I had.

He said nothing for a long time, simply watching me, and I had to resist the urge to shift around restlessly, because there was something in his eyes that made me hot. That made me aware of the throb between my legs and the tingle of my mouth where he'd kissed me.

But I couldn't think about what he'd just done to me or about that kiss. God, I could barely deal with the fact I was sitting on his bed and he was still half-naked and only inches away, let alone anything more.

Sure, you can't deal. That's why you told him he could do anything he wants to you.

Crap. I was getting myself in deeper and deeper, wasn't I?

The quilt had slipped down to his waist, leaving a whole lot of hard, sculpted muscle and tanned skin bare, along with the ink of his tattoos. And I had to fight not to drop my gaze to stare at his body.

Except looking at his face wasn't any better. His eyes glinted and his beautiful mouth curved in a way that made sweat break out all over my body. 'You'll let me do *whatever* I want?' he asked, his voice low and lazy.

'Yes.' It was difficult to say the word, but I forced it out. If that's what I had to do to get him to hide me, then I would.

The flame in his eyes burned, his smile deepening. As if he knew things I didn't. 'Yeah, I don't think you actually want that.'

'Why not?' I felt suddenly irritated at the arrogant way he seemed to think he knew things about me when he didn't. 'You have no idea what I want.'

He laughed, the sound so soft and sexy it made the breath catch in my throat. 'Baby girl, I'm an extremely dirty guy. Telling me I can do whatever I want to you is *not* something you can handle, believe me.'

I glared at him, my irritation deepening for reasons I couldn't quite explain. He was right, of course. I probably wouldn't be able to handle him. But, still, his assumption annoyed me. 'How do you know? Just because I haven't had sex before doesn't mean I can't handle it.'

'Sure you can't. That's why you pushed Crash away.'

'Yes, but that's different. I didn't want Crash.'

His eyes glinted and I realised with a start what I'd implied.

Oh, shit.

I could feel that damn blush flooding through me and I opened my mouth to tell him that didn't mean I actually wanted him, but he got in there first.

'Oh, no, don't spoil it,' he said lazily. 'And don't try to deny it either. Not that I'd believe you anyway. Not given how wet the front of my jeans still are.'

I kept my mouth closed, feeling like I was going to burst into flames with embarrassment right where I was sitting.

'It's not a big surprise anyway,' Tiger went on in that same lazy tone. 'I know you want me. You don't have to pretend otherwise. Didn't I tell you that's why you came down here in the first place?'

I wished I could have shrugged and dismissed it, or simply done what I normally do, which was not to say a word either way. Because it felt wrong that he knew what I wanted better than I did myself. Yet I couldn't seem to keep quiet. 'You're really arrogant, you know that?'

'Yes,' he said, like it was no big deal. 'I'm an asshole, too. Anything else you want to add?'

Frustrated, I looked away from him. Perhaps if I was quick, I could slide off the bed and make a break for the door. Then again, that would mean braving the guys in the hallway, and from what Tiger had said about them, perhaps I actually didn't want to do that.

Better the asshole you knew, right?

'That doesn't answer my question,' I said, changing the subject, determined to get an answer out of him one way or the other. 'Are you going to hide me or not?'

'What? In return for letting me do whatever I want to you?'

'Yes.' I made the word as definite as I could.

He was silent, his gaze roaming over me in a way that made me acutely conscious of the remains of the pleasure he'd given me, glowing inside me like hot coals, banked yet still burning. 'I'm risking a lot for you,' he murmured. 'A lot of complications. You're the chief's daughter and a virgin. A lot of shit will hit the fan if anyone found out.'

'No one will find out.' I tried to steady my voice. 'I promise I won't tell a soul.'

'Uh-huh.' His amber eyes came to mine and held them, heat flickering in them. 'Okay, then, maybe you got a deal.'

My heart leapt, relief filling me. 'Oh, that's great—'

'On one condition.'

The relief ebbed, trepidation taking its place. 'What condition?'

'Tell me you want me. And make me believe it.'

I blinked at him, not expecting it. 'Excuse me?'

'I'm thinking you need a couple of lessons in how to be strong. In how to take what you want.' The flames in his eyes leapt higher. 'Consider this your first lesson.'

Being strong starts with knowing what you want and fucking taking it...

I swallowed yet again. 'W-why do you want that?'

'Because I'm not into virgins. And unlike Crash, I'm not into having sex with girls who don't want it either.'

'Well…uh…we don't have to have sex,' I pointed out, feeling strangely disappointed in myself for doing so.

'Gotta get something in return for potentially sacrificing my club for you, baby.' Another gleam in that stare of his. 'Though I'm not sure why we're arguing about this, since you wouldn't have offered yourself if you hadn't actually wanted me to take you.'

He's right and you know it. He knows you want him, too, so what's the point in hiding it?

That was true. I just hated the vulnerability of having him know, that was the problem. The worry that he might potentially use it against me the way Dad often did. Then again, what else could I do? If I wanted him to hide me, this was the only way. Which meant I had to make it convincing.

Slowly, I shuffled over to him on my knees, and, God, even lying on his side he was intimidating. He looked at me intently, just like the big cat he shared his name with, and because he wasn't wearing a T-shirt there was nothing to hide the naked physical power of him. It was there in the hard-cut lines of his chest and stomach, and the broad width of his shoulders.

Okay, so how to convince him I wanted him? I lifted my hand to his groin.

'No,' he said before I'd even touched him, the hard, flat note in his voice freezing me in place. 'You think I'm just another cock? That a simple blow job is all it takes to convince me? Think again, baby girl.'

I met his glittering eyes, my heart thumping in my chest. He was angry—I could see that—and I wasn't sure why. Did it really matter to him whether I wanted this or not?

Of course it matters to him. He wouldn't have bothered giving you that condition otherwise.

I blinked, the realisation shocking me. I hadn't thought about him, not once. In fact, the only thing I'd thought about since I'd got here was myself. My fear and my need to hide. My desperation to avoid my dad.

But I'd made things difficult for him, hadn't I? I'd caused trouble. And asking him to hide me was going to cause him even more trouble.

Then maybe you shouldn't.

I should. I should woman up and go face my dad. And maybe if I'd been a stronger person, I would have. But I wasn't a stronger person. I was the woman who crept around not wanting to make a noise, not wanting to draw attention. Who stuck to the corners of the room rather than the centre.

The easy to manipulate target.

I couldn't stand up to my dad, not yet. But…Tiger had mentioned lessons in strength, and maybe that was worth taking. Maybe it was even worth making myself a little vulnerable for.

I stared at him, looking straight into his golden eyes, knowing he was right. That I hadn't offered myself to him simply so I could hide from Dad. Because if it had been, then I wouldn't have shoved Crash away. I would have let him do whatever he wanted to me.

But I hadn't. I'd let Tiger take me away instead and I had to admit that there was a very good reason for that. He was different. He'd always been different. He wasn't like any other man I'd met either before or since, and he'd been in my head so damn long I couldn't get him out.

I *did* want him. I'd wanted him the moment I'd met him.

I took a slow, silent breath. 'How do you want me to prove it to you then?'

'You're the genius.' Gold glinted in his gaze, a direct challenge. 'You figure it out.'

That was all very well if I'd been a genius with any experience, but I wasn't. I had no experience whatsoever except the orgasm and the kiss Tiger had given me just before.

My heart began to beat faster.

Oh, he was so close. So very, very close. All I had to do to touch him would be to reach out and I could brush fingers across the hard plane of his chest...

My palms felt sweaty, my breathing ragged, nervousness twisting inside me. And he wasn't giving me any help, simply watching me with that unblinking stare.

I was afraid and I wasn't quite sure why. Yeah, asking for what I wanted was hard for me, especially when it was often used against me. But I knew Tiger wasn't the type of guy who'd do that. He wasn't manipulative and never had been. He was straight-up. Honest. Blunt, yes, and not exactly sensitive. But he wouldn't hurt me. I'd always known that. Not the way Dad would sometimes hurt me.

So maybe feel the fear and do it anyway?

I took yet another breath, then I lifted my hands, not to make a grab for his groin this time but to cup his face between my shaking palms, his jawline hard and hot and a bit prickly against my skin.

The look in his eyes flared in surprise as I touched him, but he didn't pull away or say no this time. Instead he simply looked back, his smile gone, the expression in his gaze fierce and challenging. Daring me to make the next move.

So I did.

I bent my head and did what I'd been wanting to do since I was seventeen.

I kissed him.

His mouth was warm under mine and he didn't move, giving me no response whatsoever. I let my lips linger on his, hoping he'd take charge and show me what to do, since I had absolutely had no idea, but he didn't. He remained utterly still.

Dammit.

My pulse began to ratchet up, the heat of his skin burning against my palms. I could feel the heat of his bare chest, too, could sense the long length of his body so still and so very close to me.

He smelled *so* good.

I pressed my mouth harder against his, wanting him to do something, at least give me a hint of what to do next, but he didn't. Frustrated, I touched my tongue to his lower lip, licking at him, and finally his mouth opened and he let me in.

The taste of him hit me hard, like the kick of the bourbon I'd tried once in college. The alcohol had burned going down, which had been horrible, but then there had been a nice warm feeling in my gut afterwards, leaving my head swimming. This kiss was like both of those combined and none of it was horrible. Absolutely none of it.

I wanted more. It was like I'd discovered a brand-new addictive flavour that I couldn't get enough of. That I'd been starving for without realising it.

I held him more firmly and slid my tongue deeper into his mouth, exploring him, my whole world narrowing to the incredible heat of him and that raw, alcoholic taste.

My hands slid into his short dark copper-tinted hair, all thick and silky against my fingers, the way I'd always guessed it would be. And… *God*, he tasted good. I moaned helplessly, deep in my throat, wanting more yet not knowing what more I wanted. All that mattered was that I got more of *him*.

Except he still wasn't moving and it was driving me crazy.

Then suddenly I felt his fingers wrap around my wrists and he was pulling my hands from his hair and drawing back from me, leaving me panting and shaking, my lips feeling hot and tingly and my mouth full of his intoxicating flavour.

The amber colour of his eyes had turned into molten gold, gleaming and hot, and I could feel myself begin to catch fire right where I knelt.

'W-well?' I asked shakily, my voice thick. 'Was I convincing enough?'

That beautiful mouth I'd just tasted curved. 'No.'

'Tiger—'

'You can finish convincing me back at my place. Where we've got a bit more privacy.' Abruptly, he let go my wrists and rolled out of bed, reaching for his T-shirt and leather vest, then pausing to put on his boots.

I sat there watching him, my heart pumping furiously, full of the weirdest combination of emotions. Excited. Thrilled. Afraid. Desperate. Angry. Wanting.

I didn't like it. I'd never been comfortable with extremes of emotion and I didn't know what to do with all those extremes now. What I wanted was to crawl under the quilt and pretend I was back at home, that I hadn't come down to the Knights of Ruin's clubhouse purely on a stupid, cowardly whim.

But it was too late. I was getting myself deeper and deeper into trouble with every passing minute.

Tiger finished with his boots and stood up, glancing down at me, reading me perfectly. 'Second thoughts?'

I couldn't deny it. 'Y-yes.'

He held out his hand to me. 'Come on. I promise it'll be okay.' Then he smiled and just like that, everything fell away.

No one had ever smiled at me like that before, with real warmth, like a ray of sunlight on a midwinter day. It probably meant nothing. Maybe it was simply his normal, average 'Hi, how are ya?' smile.

But it felt like a kick to the chest, jolting me all the way through.

Sure, it might simply have been because he was going to get laid and that would make any guy smile—or so I'd heard.

But suddenly I didn't care. He'd given that smile to *me*. That gorgeous, incredible smile was *mine*. And I knew I'd do anything to get him to give it to me again.

So I took his hand and let his warm fingers wrap around mine.

And then I let him take me away.

CHAPTER EIGHT

Tiger

I MADE SURE Summer's hoodie was pulled over her head as I stepped out into the corridor once again. The orgy was still going on, this time with a different combination of people, but once again I ignored what was going on, pulling Summer with me as I strode past.

Again, a couple of the brothers yelled at me to join in, but I ignored them, too. All I wanted was to get Summer out of there as quickly and with as little fuss as possible.

I couldn't stop thinking about that fucking kiss she'd laid on me, though.

I knew she wanted me, it was fucking obvious, but what I'd wanted was for her to admit it. I wasn't going to take her back to my place and do whatever the fuck I wanted with her if she wasn't into it. Then again, I'd been the one who'd wanted something in return for hiding her from her dad.

I shouldn't have insisted. If all I'd wanted was pussy, then I could have let her go and got all the pussy I wanted right here, right now, and with way fewer complications.

But the fucking annoying thing was that I didn't just want any pussy.

I wanted *her* pussy in particular.

So when she'd offered herself to me… Christ, I hadn't been able to get it out of my head. I shouldn't have encouraged her. I should have told her no. Kept on spouting that bullshit about how I wasn't the right guy for a little virgin like her.

Except I hadn't. I'd let her offer herself, let her push it. And now here we were, going down the corridor to the entrance to the club, because apparently my dick was doing my thinking for me.

Of course I didn't stop walking, though, my head full of that goddamn kiss and my heart racing like I'd spent all day in the fucking gym.

When I'd told her I wanted her to convince me, all I'd wanted was some sign that she was into it. But when she'd gone for my cock like every other club girl, for some reason I'd just felt…angry.

I had no idea why it mattered so much that her attention should be about me, but it had. Then she'd looked at me with those big blue eyes, like I was an ice cream she was desperate to taste. And she'd taken my face between her hands, and bent her head, putting that soft, pretty little mouth on mine.

Her kiss had been so shy and unpractised, and it shouldn't have lit me up inside like a fucking match to a skyrocket. I didn't like that kind of innocent shit.

But there was something about the way Summer

looked at me, about the way she kissed me, that stole the air from my lungs.

I wanted to take her home. I wanted to get her naked. I wanted to do every dirty thing to her that I could think of and then I wanted to do it again.

Hiding her, having her, was going to complicate the fuck out of things and for someone who didn't like complicated, that was a problem. But when I wanted something, I didn't like to deny myself.

Shit, apart from anything else, I wanted to get to the bottom of whatever was going on with her fucking father, because hearing her talk about him gave me a bad feeling. And if there was one thing I didn't like it was a bad feeling.

I pulled Summer past the prospect guarding the clubhouse entrance, then went down the steps outside to where all the rides were parked up.

My buddy Smoke was in the process of helping Cat, his old lady, get off his bike as I approached mine, and he lifted his chin in acknowledgement.

Smoke glanced at Summer, then down at our joined hands. 'Who's this?' he asked, raising a brow. 'Anyone special?'

Even though Smoke was my best friend, I knew what he'd think about me hiding Summer. Or screwing Summer. Or doing anything at all with Summer. So I gave him my usual shit-eating grin. 'Nope. Just some fun.'

Cat came up beside Smoke and gave me a cool look.

Cat and I had had our differences. She'd never liked the club or me, and I'd always thought she'd treated Smoke like shit, not to mention being judgey as hell. But since she and Smoke had got together, she'd mellowed. Though not enough to approve of what I was doing now with Summer, that was for sure.

And that was another thing I should have remembered. Cat had shacked up with Summer's brother for a time, even had a kid with him, so if there was anyone who'd recognise Summer, it was her.

Fuck. I needed to get out of here and fast.

'Going to join the orgy?' I asked her conversationally, when it didn't seem like they were going to leave without a chat. 'Looks like everyone's having a great time.'

Cat sighed. 'An orgy. My favourite.' She looked at Smoke. 'Can we go home now, please?'

Smoke shot me a 'fuck you, asshole' glance before starting the placating process. Poor bastard.

My work done, I quickly grabbed Summer and lifted her onto my bike. There was a helmet in the saddlebags that I took out and put on her head, straight over the top of her hoodie. Then, wasting no time, I got on myself, fired up the engine, then lit on out of there.

Summer didn't make a sound, but her hands abruptly came down on my hips as the bike took off, and her body leaned into mine. I could feel the warmth of her settled against my back as if she'd done this a thousand times before, which was weird. I'd given her a couple of rides while I'd been guarding her and I seemed to remember her almost falling off because she hadn't wanted to hold on to me.

Apparently she had no problems with it now and, fuck, neither did I.

She was hot and her bare thighs spread on either side of mine felt insanely good. And the feel of her fit in perfectly with the usual thrill I got out of riding. With the freedom of it.

I didn't like the thought, though, didn't like the way it tightened in my chest, so I ignored it, opening the throttle and going faster instead.

My place wasn't anything fancy, just an old warehouse building that had been converted. I had the bottom floor, which suited me fine, because it gave me a ton of room for a workshop where I could work on my bikes.

I liked dicking around with engines and parts. I liked taking them apart and putting them back together again. I liked making shit go. An engine was simply a giant puzzle and I'd always liked puzzles, even back when I was a kid.

Couldn't read, but give me a Rubik's cube and I could solve that motherfucker in ten seconds flat.

I rode straight up to the automatic roller door at the back of the building and pressed the button to open it—I'd rigged up an automatic door opener since I hated getting off my bike to open fucking doors—then I rode straight inside.

The whole place was just a wide-open space, with a few walls to separate off the bathroom and a set of iron stairs that led to a mezzanine where I had my bed. Down one end of the giant room was a kitchen—simple, like me—and down the other was the workshop, with a big workbench that ran along the wall and lots of shelves above it. I had a few bikes parked up—the brothers often got me to work on theirs—and there was one up on a stand.

In the middle of the room was a couch and a couple of chairs as a living area, plus a huge-ass TV—I liked movies and plenty of the brothers had enjoyed the odd football game around here, too.

Parking the bike down the workshop end, I kicked down the stand and got off, turning to help Summer. She was fiddling with her helmet, trying to get it undone, but I knocked her hands away and pulled it off for her. She blinked up at me, her hood falling back and revealing her face, all pink and pretty, and her pale hair spread over her shoulders.

My groin ached, my fucking dick reminding me that it was impatient and now she was here, in my territory, I could do whatever the hell I wanted with her.

Starting fucking now.

'Lift your arms,' I ordered and her arms came up just like that, as if she'd been born to obey my orders.

My cock got even harder.

I saw belated realisation cross her face about what she was doing, but by that stage it was too late. I already had my hands on her hoodie and I was pulling it up and over her head, then dropping it to the floor. Finally getting to see what she was wearing under all that cotton.

And, fuck me, I nearly had a heart attack.

All she had on was the tiniest, tightest, stretchiest blue crop top in the entire history of the world. It left a whole lot of the pale skin of her stomach on show and pulled tight across a pair of small, perfectly rounded little tits. It also left her shoulders bare and I found myself fascinated by the delicate shape of her collarbones and by the hollow of her throat where her pulse was beating hard and fast.

She wasn't wearing a bra, her hard nipples obvious through the fabric of her top, a fact she clearly had no idea about since she made no effort to cover them. Instead, she glanced away from me, looking curiously around at the apartment like a kid in a toy shop.

I didn't usually bring chicks back here and the few times I had, it wasn't my place they were interested in, not when they could get their hands on my cock. But not Summer apparently, and it put me off guard. Made me feel…uncomfortable, as if she could see things about me just from my place that I wasn't ready to show anyone.

'Wow,' she murmured, staring at my workbench, her eyes widening. 'You've got a workshop in your apartment. How cool.'

Oh, no, I didn't want her getting interested. Not now.

I reached out and put a finger under her chin, urging her gaze back to mine. 'Nice distraction, but I'm up here.'

Pools of wide, dark blue hit me hard, like a sucker punch, and for a second all I could do was stare back.

I was standing very close to her, those pretty tits almost brushing my chest, and that innocent, flowery scent was doing things to me it shouldn't. Like getting me even harder than I was already.

I'd planned to get her comfortable here first before we moved onto anything else, but after making her come back in the clubhouse, I honestly wasn't sure I could wait. Which was a massive fucking first.

Reaching into my pocket, I grabbed my phone and hit Keep's number. 'Prez, it's me,' I said when he answered. 'I'm out looking for her. Let you know if I see anything.' I didn't wait for him to speak, I simply hit Disconnect before he could say a word, then pocketed the phone again.

Summer swallowed and looked away from me before glancing back. Yeah, she was nervous. I could see her trembling. 'S-so,' she said uncertainly. 'What do we do—'

'Quiet.' I lifted a hand and gently rubbed my thumb along her full lower lip in a slow back and forth.

She took a sharp breath, stiffening as I touched her. I could see she wanted to pull away, but she was trapped by the bike behind her and me in front of her.

Poor baby girl. Nowhere to run to this time.

I didn't give her any space and I didn't stop touching her lip, the soft give of it under my thumb such a damn turn-on. I'd never bothered to take my time with a woman before, mainly because the club girls all tended to be as impatient as I was when it came to fucking. But it turned out that just running my thumb across Summer's silky skin made me as breathless as being balls-deep in club pussy, so Christ knew what was going to happen to me when I actually did get inside her.

'You're shaking,' I said after a moment. 'That me?

You afraid?' I didn't like that idea. She shouldn't be afraid, and definitely not of me.

'N-no.' The stutter in her husky voice revealed the lie that it was.

'Bullshit.' I pressed down on her lip slightly. 'Gimme the truth, baby.'

She took another sharp breath, her blue eyes coming to mine. 'Okay. Yes. A little. But not…not the way you think.'

'Uh-huh. So what then?'

'I just…' Her lashes fluttered. 'It's only that I've wanted you since I was seventeen.'

This time it was my turn to stare at her, my thumb pausing on her mouth, feeling like I'd taken not only that punch to the gut but a kick to the head, as well.

Seventeen? She'd wanted me since she'd been *seventeen*?

Holy fucking shit.

'I know, it's stupid,' she went on, the words coming out of her in a rush. 'But I thought you were… amazing. You weren't like any other guy I'd ever met, dangerous and mean and hot. And I…I'm afraid, Tiger. I'm afraid I won't be able to handle you. But I want to. You've been in my head for so long and I can't… I just…' She trailed off, blushing, clearly embarrassed by what she'd said, looking away from me yet again.

For a second I wasn't sure how I felt about that and then I realised that of course I knew how I felt about it.

I fucking loved it.

I'd been in her head all that time. Five goddamn years and all she'd been thinking about was me.

'Hey,' I growled softly, urging her gaze back to mine. 'Do you trust me?' A dumb fucking question when I'd never done anything to earn her trust, but I had to ask her all the same.

She took a second, but only one before she nodded. And that got to me, too, couldn't deny it. Been a long time since a civilian had trusted me, not since Mom and Tommy. The brothers, sure, that was a given, but everyone else? Nope. Not that I'd given a fuck about a civilian's trust, not when they didn't exactly figure in my life, but this one right here? Yeah, hers mattered.

'Don't worry about whether you can handle me or not,' I went on, starting up that caress on her bottom lip again. 'I know you can. But we're gonna take this nice and slow to start with. Everything I do is supposed to feel good, so if it doesn't, you let me know, okay?'

She gave a little shiver. 'Okay.'

'Good.' I let my finger trail down from her lip, over that stubborn chin and down over the soft skin of her neck and throat to her collarbones, tracing the shapes of them lightly.

She inhaled, goosebumps rising all over her skin wherever I touched her, the pale, creamy colour of it beginning to flush pink.

'Fuck, you're sensitive.' I slid my finger just underneath the neckline of that stretchy blue crop top, stroking the warm silky skin of her chest in another slow back and forth. 'I love it.'

Her cheeks began to glow, the blue of her eyes darkening as I stroked her, and I couldn't take my gaze off her face as the effects of my touch began to take hold. Christ, it was addictive watching her get aroused. Knowing that it was me doing this to her, that no one else had ever made her feel this way.

'So, what's with the virgin thing?' I didn't stop stroking her, back and forth beneath the fabric of her top, grazing the tops of her pretty tits. 'Never met a guy you really liked or what?'

'Well…yeah.' Her voice had got even huskier and breathless sounding. 'Plus, I'm just not very good with people.'

'Are you sure? Maybe it's that people aren't very good with you.'

Her lashes fell, hiding all that blue from me. 'I don't mind. I don't much like people anyway.'

'But you like me.' I hooked my finger into the neckline of her top and tugged gently, testing to see how much it would stretch. 'I think you like me a lot.'

She took a ragged breath, glancing up at me, then away again, shifting restlessly on her feet. 'M-maybe.'

Didn't take a genius to figure out why she was moving around like that. Or why her nipples were pressing in stiff little points against the material of her top.

It was definitely time to take this up a notch.

CHAPTER NINE

Summer

TIGER WAS STANDING so close I could barely breathe. He was so tall and his shoulders were so wide; he was like a wall right in front of me. A wall made of hard muscle and covered with tanned skin and ink, with a layer of cotton and leather thrown over it.

And he was touching me. He had the tip of his finger inside the neckline of my top and was slowly stroking me back and forth. It felt like he was painting me with flame, leaving scorch marks all over my skin.

Not that I could look down to check, not with the way he was watching me. So carefully and intently, as if he was fascinated by what he saw in my face.

I'd never had someone look at me like that before. It made my heartbeat do that thumping thing again, and made my skin too hot and too tight. I felt like I wanted to rip it right off or climb right out of it.

I shouldn't have told him all that stuff about how long I'd wanted him, not straight out like that, but I hadn't been able to stop myself. He'd asked me if I was afraid and I didn't want him to think that I was, but the truth had slipped out all the same. Along with my pathetic confession.

I'd had no idea how he would take it, but I really hadn't expected the look of satisfaction that had gleamed in his eyes. As if he'd liked the idea of me lusting after him, and liked it a lot.

I hadn't expected him to ask me whether I trusted him either, and I was even more surprised when I found myself nodding almost instantly. But then maybe it wasn't such a surprise. Tiger had never hurt me, never manipulated me. Sure, he'd teased me but it had never been malicious or cruel. And it had only made me feel irritated, not hurt.

So, yeah, I trusted him, and the fact that he'd even asked me had eased my nervousness somewhat, but now, with that finger tracing patterns on me, it was all flooding back again full force.

I hadn't been expecting for him to get straight to the sex part of the evening. I'd thought we might talk for a bit or watch TV or have a drink or something first. And I wouldn't have minded looking around his apartment, because the minute we'd ridden inside, I'd known it wasn't like any other apartment I'd ever seen before and I was curious.

But then he'd caged me against his bike and had taken my hoodie off and right then and there, I knew he wasn't going to wait.

Perhaps I should have been flattered with his impatience. Then again, it wasn't really me he wanted, was it? It was what I'd promised him. The sex.

Something that felt an awful lot like disappointment shifted inside me, but I didn't give it any time to sit there. Of course this wasn't about me; it never had been. So I should just enjoy what was happening and the fact that after so many years, I was finally going to get what I wanted. Him.

If I didn't completely freak the hell out first.

He tugged my top again, his amber gaze gleaming as it dropped to where the fabric stretched over my breasts. 'Hmm. I think I see something that wants to be touched.'

I glanced down, too, wanting to see what he was talking about, and then, with a jolt, understood. My nipples were hard and were pressing very obviously against the thin material.

Full of embarrassment, I raised my hands to cover myself, but he grabbed my wrists and held them down at my sides. 'No, don't do that. Just keep them there, okay?'

I gave a shaky nod, because I'd told him I trusted him and I did.

Releasing my wrists, he hooked the fingers of both hands into the stretchy fabric of my top and began to ease it down my upper arms. Though it had sleeves, the neckline was supposed to leave my shoulders bare, but now Tiger was pulling it down further so it stretched tight across my chest, binding my arms to my sides. And he didn't stop, pulling the fabric down so that it slid over my acutely sensitive nipples and off, baring my breasts completely.

I hadn't put a bra on underneath it, because the girls that usually went to the clubhouse didn't wear them either, but I'd forgotten that fact since I'd had the hoodie on over the top. But I was acutely aware of it now, a sharp, ragged breath escaping me as cool air washed over my heated skin.

The instinct to cover myself was almost overwhelming, but the way he'd pulled my top down made it impossible for me to lift my arms.

'Well, look at you,' Tiger breathed, his eyes deep gold as he stared down at my naked breasts. 'Absolutely fucking perfect tits.' He lifted his hands, cupping me, his big warm palms on my aching flesh making me shudder.

His gaze came to mine again, watching me as his thumbs moved to slowly circle my throbbing nipples. He knew what he was doing to me, no question, not that there was any way for me to hide it. Not when his touch drew a gasp from my throat and sent a hot jolt of electricity straight between my thighs. He circled his thumbs again and again, then brushed them right over the hard tips of my breasts, studying me the whole time like the predator he was.

I shuddered, my brain slowly shutting down as a hot, molten feeling grew between my thighs. 'Tiger,' I said shakily, feeling suddenly unsure about what was happening.

No one had touched me like this before and his fingers on my skin were like flames. It made me afraid that I'd been right all along. That I wasn't going to be able to handle him. I was so inexperienced and this was so new and I…and I…

'Hey.' His voice somehow caught my flailing attention, calling it back. 'Look at me.'

An arm slid around my waist, easing me close so

my body was pressed right up against the hard, hot length of his. I hadn't realised until that moment how weak my knees had got until I found myself leaning against him, as if I needed him to hold me up.

My bare breasts grazed his chest, the cotton of his T-shirt rubbing against my nipples, drawing yet another shudder from me and making my breath catch.

He held me tight, his free hand catching my chin and tilting my face up so I was looking right into his eyes. 'Remember. This is all supposed to feel good, okay?'

He was so hot and hard. Solid and muscular. Reassuring and protective. I felt as if I could lean all my weight on him and he wouldn't let go or drop me. He'd let me lean against him forever, holding me tightly so I wouldn't fall.

'I know,' I managed to get out. 'And it does. But I've never done this before and it's so new. I...I don't know what to do with myself.'

That beautiful, sexy, delicious mouth curved in a smile that took the rest of my breath away. 'You don't have to do anything with yourself. All you have to do is relax and let me do the rest. You can do that, can't you?' There it was again, that look in his eyes, that challenge. The dare that made me want to put back my shoulders and show him that of course I could do it. I could take whatever he threw at me and then some.

'You want me, though?' The words came out before I could think better of them. 'I mean me. Not one of the club girls, right?'

He frowned, searching my face, his eyes full of

amber heat. 'I told you I was a dirty guy, and I meant it. Nothing I like better than a full-on fucking orgy. But did you see me stop in the hallway in the club- house? Did you see me even look?'

I shook my head slowly, remembering that he hadn't.

'No, because I didn't.' He let go of my chin and grabbed one of my hands, drawing my palm directly over the hard, thick ridge behind his zipper. 'This is for you. This is *all* for you. Understand me?'

I caught my breath, feeling the length and breadth of him beneath my palm. So hard and getting even harder. I was doing this to him, wasn't I? This was me.

As if that reassurance was exactly what I needed to hear, the uncertainty inside me began to recede, leaving behind it a kind of wonder. At myself and my own power. A power I hadn't ever explored before or even realised I had.

If I could do this to him, what else could I do?

But Tiger didn't give me any time to think about it. He picked me up as though I weighed absolutely nothing at all and turned, carrying me over to the battered leather couch in the living area and setting me down on it.

I tried to raise my arms again, but my top was holding them tightly to my sides and I couldn't move. He didn't seem to think this was a problem and took no notice of my wriggles to try to free them. Instead he eased me back into the corner of the couch, be- tween the arm and the back of it, positioning me so my legs were stretched along the cushions and he was kneeling astride them. Then he put his hands on my thighs and pushed the stupid denim mini right up to my waist.

I tensed, shivering, because now he was looking down right between my thighs, and the expression on his face had got even more intense. 'Hmm. What do we have here?' He reached out and brushed his fingers lightly over the front of my panties, making me jerk and gasp as if he'd electrocuted me. 'White cotton. Very pretty. Very innocent.' His fingers moved again, tracing the outline of my sex through the fabric as he lifted his hot gaze to mine. 'And very, very wet.'

My face felt like it was going to burst into flames for the millionth time that night, heat like the backdraft from some massive fire washing over me. I wanted to bend my knees, hide myself somehow, but the way he was kneeling meant I couldn't, and with my arms bound to my sides, I couldn't even push my skirt down.

Except I was supposed to be dealing with the challenge of him, right? Not getting shivery and scared the way I had back in the clubhouse.

So I made myself stare back, ignoring how vulnerable I felt with my top bunched under my bare breasts and my skirt pushed up around my waist.

He grinned and I thought I saw approval in his eyes, which made a hot glow start up in my chest. But then he stroked me again, and the hot glow turned into short sharp spikes of pleasure.

'I know,' he said lazily, sliding the tip of his finger under the cotton of my panties an inch, teasing me. 'You don't like having your top pulled down like that, do you? Well, sorry, baby, but I don't want you touching me just yet. And I don't want you covering yourself either.' He stroked along the edge of the cotton, over the incredibly sensitive skin at the crease of my thigh. 'I want to play with you without your hands in getting in the way.'

I shook as that teasing finger stroked over the front of my panties yet again. 'But I—'

'Quiet,' he ordered, glancing down between my thighs again. 'I want to get a look at this little pussy.' He leaned over me, one hand braced on the couch cushions beside my hip while with the other he pulled aside cotton, baring me.

I squirmed, uncomfortable with the intent way he was studying me and with the way I was exposed, bound and helpless. But he ignored me, smoothing his fingers over the slick flesh of my sex instead. 'Nice.' His voice was warm with approval as I stiffened in response, gasping as another hard spike of pleasure jolted the length of my spine. 'Pretty curls and so pink. So wet.' His fingers slid over me again, tearing a groan from my throat. 'Is that all for me, baby girl? Are you all wet for me?'

I could barely hear him. His fingers had found my clit and he was circling it, his strokes slow and firm, the pleasure making my head tip back against the arm of the couch and my eyes close tightly.

Ohmigod. *So* good.

'I'm looking for an answer. Come on, tell me.'

'Y-yes,' I gasped. 'It's all…for you.'

'Yeah, it's all fucking mine, isn't it?' He gave my

clit a flick and I almost sobbed at the intensity of the pleasure that lanced through me. 'Just the way I like it.'

My nails were digging into my palms and I couldn't keep still, my hips shifting restlessly as that finger resumed circling again and again. I was desperate to spread my legs but he had his knees on either side of mine so I couldn't, and that hint of re-straint somehow made everything ten thousand times hotter and me ten thousand times more impatient.

'Tiger,' I groaned. 'Please…move. I want to…'

'Not yet.' He brought his knees together, holding my thighs even more tightly closed, and then he put both hands down on either side of my hips, bending down low over me. I could feel the warmth of his breath against my wet flesh and my brain seemed to freeze.

God, was he really going to…?

Then I felt it, his tongue on me as he gave me a long slow lick straight up the centre of my pussy.

I went rigid, pleasure exploding the length of my body, a choked cry escaping me. Tiger only made a low, rumbling satisfied sound. 'Fuck, you taste good.' Then he licked me again. And again.

I shuddered, writhing beneath him, my aware-ness narrowing down to the lash of his tongue be-tween my legs and the almost unbearable pleasure that came along with it. And it only got worse as he wrapped his arms around my hips, holding on to me and burying his face between my thighs.

I gave a hoarse scream, even more desperate to move, to spread my legs so his tongue could get to the place where I needed more pressure, more friction, more…something. But he was holding them closed and even though the way he was licking me was pushing me nearer and nearer to orgasm, it wasn't quite enough to push me over completely.

I sobbed in frustration, my hips shifting as he toyed with me, as he licked me, as he used his fingers on me. And it was only when I was begging, babbling and incoherent, that he concentrated his tongue on my clit, a relentless pressure that eventually pushed me over the edge, making pleasure explode like a bomb inside me, my screams so loud that the room echoed with them.

Afterwards I lay there, boneless and heavy, not wanting to move or even open my eyes. I could feel his weight on me shift, his hands on my thighs, spreading them finally wide apart.

I groaned, a different, luxurious kind of pleasure rolling through me, as he positioned me, hooking one leg over the arm of the couch while pushing wide the other.

Then his fingers were on my pussy again, spreading my wet flesh apart, and he was back, licking and exploring me relentlessly.

I twisted, panting, trying to avoid his clever tongue, but he held me still, made me take it. 'It's too much,' I protested weakly, writhing. 'I can't…'

'Yes, you can.' His breath was hot against my sensitive skin. 'I want you wet, baby. Really, really wet.'

'I think I'm wet enough already.'

He laughed, a deep, rough, sexy sound. 'No, you're not. Besides, I fucking love eating you out. Deal with it.'

I didn't know if I could deal with it to be honest, especially when I couldn't do anything with my hands.

'Look at me,' he said, as if he knew I was having trouble.

And idiot that I was, I did. And as soon as I opened my eyes I knew it had been a mistake to look because the sight of him lying between my spread thighs hit me like a punch to the gut.

His gaze was molten and feral, gleaming and hungry, and as I met it, his fingers slid through my slick folds, toying lazily with me and watching me as he did so, taking in every shudder, hearing every desperate moan.

It was unbearably erotic.

'You wanted to handle me? So handle me.' He slid one finger slowly inside me, the smooth glide of it making me shudder and sweat. 'Handle me, playing with your pussy and making you watch.' He slid another finger in beside the first, stretching me gently.

I tried to say something, but I couldn't think of what words to say. The sight of him with his hand on me, his fingers disappearing inside me, made everything vanish.

He pumped his fingers, sliding them in and out, slow and deep. 'You're really tight, baby girl. But you feel so good. I can't wait to get inside you.'

I couldn't stop shaking, my body already starting to get desperate again, and I couldn't drag my gaze from his, lost in all that gold.

He kept playing with me as if he had all the time in the world and then he added his tongue again, exploring me once more with a relentlessness that had me sobbing.

It was only then that he moved away, kneeling upright on the couch cushions and grabbing his wallet out of his back pocket. He took out a condom packet, tossed the wallet on the floor, then ripped open the foil without any hurry. Then he unzipped his fly and reached down to get out his cock. Gripping it in one hand, he casually rolled down the condom with the other.

I couldn't remember whether I'd seen a naked dick before or not, but right now my brain wasn't working. At all. Then again, it didn't matter whether I'd seen one before or not, since the only dick that mattered was Tiger's.

God, he was big. Really, really big. And long and thick.

My fingers itched. I wanted to touch him, to see what he felt like. To see whether he was as smooth and as hot and as hard as he looked.

Except he wasn't going to give me a chance, that much was obvious as he finished with the condom and moved forward to kneel between my thighs. The smile and the laziness had vanished, a raw, hungry light in his eyes.

He slid one big hand beneath my butt, lifting me up a little, while with the other he gripped his cock, rubbing the head of it through the wet flesh of my pussy. I groaned, electricity sparking, making me arch up into him.

'Fuck, I want you,' he breathed, a strange note in his voice. As if he was shocked by the fact. 'What

the hell are you doing to me, baby girl?' He searched
my face like he was looking for answers. 'Straight
vanilla fucking and I'm almost ready to come. This
is not normal for me, understand?'

I didn't know what he wanted me to say, but then
I wasn't thinking straight, not while I could feel the
head of his dick nudging against my clit, making
me jerk and shudder like I was holding on to a bare
electrical wire.

'Christ, you're hot.' He slid the head of his cock
down the length of my pussy, finding my entrance
and pushing lightly. 'I don't want to hurt you, so I'll
try and go easy.' He pushed again and I heard his
breath catch along with my own as my flesh parted
around him. 'Holy *fuck…*' he whispered, staring
down at me, his amber eyes darkening. 'You feel
insanely good.'

He began to push into me, slow and steady, leaving me no time to be scared, no time to doubt. No
time to pull away or change my mind. I was so wet
there was no resistance and the only pain I felt was a
slight pinch. It was more the unfamiliarity of it that
made me tremble, that made me gasp. The stretch and
burn of my sex around his as he invaded me. Filled
me. 'Tiger…' My voice shook. 'Oh, my God… Tiger.'

He kept on going, kept on pushing, steady, relentless, his golden eyes all I could see. And when
he was finally all inside me, as deep as he could go,
he paused, his gaze still pinning mine. He had one
hand on the arm of the couch, the other on the back,
and I could hear the harsh sound of his breathing.

And I knew—I just *knew*—that this was affecting

him as much as it was affecting me. I could hear it in his breathing and in the look of shock in his eyes. He was staring at me as if he'd never seen anything like me before in his entire life.

'Summer.' The way he said my name went through me like a knife and I wasn't sure why. There was a note of something in it, like wonder, and it made me feel like crying all of a sudden. Then he said it again, *'Summer,'* harsher this time, and he drew his hips back, thrusting into me.

I wanted my hands free. I wanted to touch him but I couldn't. I could only lie there and watch the flames leap in his gaze, getting hotter and rawer as he moved.

Another deep thrust and the orgasm swept over me so unexpectedly that I didn't even have time to scream, conscious only of the pleasure detonating inside me, leaving me writhing. Then another one began to build, and I think I sobbed, because I wasn't sure I could survive. Because if this was what sex was all about then I was ruined. Destroyed.

But something inside me knew that all sex wasn't like this. That it was only like this because of him. Because of Tiger.

Because he was the one who'd destroyed me and kept on destroying me with every thrust of his hips, every gasp he drew from me, every sob.

He began to move faster, harder, shifting his hold and gripping my hips, showing me how to move with him. Then he angled his thrusts so he hit my clit every time he sank into me and I was gone.

I didn't scream this time, only sobbed.

As I came apart in his hands.

CHAPTER TEN

Tiger

I KNEW THE moment she came, could feel her tight little pussy clamp down hard on my cock, gripping me like a fist. And I don't know what happened, but a hot rush of pleasure flooded through me, and I realised that instead of the hours it normally took me to get off, I was on the verge of coming already, even though I'd only just got inside her.

It didn't make any sense. There shouldn't have been any reason why I suddenly felt at the edge of my control. I wasn't a teenage boy and this wasn't my first fuck. This was a virgin and straight out missionary, and yet if I didn't get myself under control, I was going to lose it on virtually the first couple of thrusts.

I had no idea what was wrong with me.

She was laid out underneath me, her head back against the corner of the couch, her eyes closed, her mouth open. Strands of hair were sticking to her neck and I could see sweat beading on her forehead where more strands of hair were sticking. Her cheeks were deeply flushed and there was a trail of moisture out of the corner of one eye.

She looked so fucking beautiful, so fucking sexy. She looked wrecked and I was the one who'd wrecked her. And I wasn't even sorry. I hadn't even come yet and I wanted to wreck her again and again. And maybe wreck myself along with her.

Fuck, where had all of this come from? I wanted to pull away, because if there was one thing I hated, it was feeling uncomfortable, but the ache in my dick wouldn't let me.

Jesus, she was so tight. And hot. And wet. And she smelled of sex and flowers. And the way she was lying there, all abandoned, was driving me insane.

There was no fighting this. I was going to come and come hard.

I thrust again, harder, pushing deep into her pussy, gripping her hips in my hands. She shuddered and her back arched, and before I knew what I was doing, I was moving faster, even harder. Slamming myself into her. Losing myself in the feel of her tight pussy around my cock.

Then, just before I lost it completely, she opened her eyes and looked up at me, and it was like I'd fallen into the depths of the sea, nothing but dark blue all around me.

She said my name, very softly, in that husky voice and, fuck, it sent me straight over the edge.

I bent and kissed her savagely, roaring into her mouth as the orgasm hit me like a fucking baseball bat, my hips thrusting wildly, out of control and not giving a shit as pleasure exploded inside me like a goddamn nuclear bomb.

Not thinking straight, I loosened my grip on the couch and leaned forward, gathering her up and pulling her into my lap so her legs were around my waist. Then I turned my head into her damp neck, inhaling that sexy scent of hers, breathing it in and trying to calm myself the fuck down.

I was still inside her, though, and I could feel my cock slowly hardening yet again. Jesus, I'd barely got this round down and already I was up for another.

Even though I didn't want to, I pulled out of her, loving how she gave a delicate little shudder as I did so. 'Be right back,' I murmured, releasing her and letting her slide down onto the cushions. I got off the couch and went into the kitchen area, getting rid of the condom in the trash before coming back to her, pulling off my clothes as I went.

I'd left hers on because I liked the half dressed, half naked look, but now I wanted nothing between us but skin.

Those big blue eyes opened wide as I kicked my boots off, then peeled my T-shirt up and over my head, then shucked my jeans and underwear. Gave me a fucking huge thrill the way she was looking at me, not hiding the fact that she liked what she saw. Most women did and, shit, what man didn't like that?

But there was something about the way this little girl was staring that made me hard instantly, and when her gaze dropped to my dick, I got even harder.

'Time to get naked, baby girl.' I stalked over to the couch and her eyes were like goddamn saucers as I reached down and pulled her top off. Then I got rid of her miniskirt and her panties, too.

Once she was finally bare, I laid her down flat on the cushions, then I eased myself over her the way I had back in my room in the clubhouse, her warm little body beneath mine, my hips resting between her thighs and that hot little pussy right against my dick.

I braced myself on my elbows on either side of her head, leaning down to nuzzle her neck, licking her throat to get another taste of the salt on her skin. I wanted to spread her thighs and bury my face in her pussy again, but I figured she'd need some recovery time. I hadn't gone easy on her, that was for sure.

She shivered as my tongue touched her throat, and I felt her palms press against my chest.

Yeah, I really hadn't gone easy on her.

I lifted my head. 'You okay? Not sore?'

'Tender maybe, but not sore, no.' Her hands slid from my chest up to my shoulders, her fingers spreading out. 'I want to touch you. Can I?'

'Baby, you don't need to ask permission. But right now, since I'm already pretty fucking hard and you need a break, I don't think that's a good idea.'

She sighed. 'Maybe you're right. So…you said you liked orgies and being dirty. Does that mean that later you want to…um…you know, with me?'

It was obvious what she meant and, prick that I was, I just had to tease her about it. 'What? You want some group sex? Well, sure. If you're into it we could—'

'No!' She gave me a slap on the shoulder, which I found weirdly hot. 'I definitely do *not* want group sex.'

I grinned, putting her out of her misery. 'Good.

Because as of now, I've decided I don't like sharing.'
The addition *what's mine* echoed inside my head,
but I managed not to say it aloud. Because it was
fucking strange enough that I found the thought of
sharing her vaguely enraging, let alone thinking of
her as mine.

Hell, I'd only been with her a few hours and it
was way too soon to be thinking about shit like that.
If ever.

'That's okay then.' She gave me a stern look,
absently stroking my shoulder. 'I don't want to be
shared.'

My brothers getting their filthy hands on her…
Yeah, I did *not* like that thought. At all. 'Don't worry.
There's plenty of other dirty things we can do that
don't involve other people.' The way her hand was
moving on my shoulder made me want to shiver,
which was just flat out fucking weird. No one
touched me gently like that and I wasn't sure I liked
it. Trying to ignore the feeling, I grinned. 'You leave
the dirty part to me, okay?'

She gave me a solemn nod. 'Okay.'

Jesus. She was fucking adorable.

Her gaze dropped to the shoulder she was touching, her fingers beginning to trace my ink. 'By the
way, this tattoo is incredible. I love all the angles and
stuff. Where did you find the design?'

I shrugged. 'Drew it myself. I liked it so I thought
I'd get it inked.'

She gave me a startled glance. 'You did? Because
wow.'

That look in her eyes. Christ. Like I was something

amazing she'd never seen before, which only made
me more uncomfortable.

I tried to brush it off. 'It's just a tattoo.'

'No, it's not.' Her finger traced one of the circles.
'Look at it. The way this spiral interlocks with the
others. And the circles here and all the arcs… It's
beautiful, Tiger.' She glanced up at me again, blue
glowing in her eyes. But it wasn't anger this time.
In fact, it looked a hell of a lot like…interest. 'I love
the geometries in it.' She gave an odd little smile
that made something kick hard in my chest. 'Math
is kind of my thing and I love it when everything—
I don't know—just fits.'

'Like parts in an engine.' Shit, why I had said
that? Chicks didn't like talking about engine parts.
At least not the chicks I talked to. Not that I did much
talking with them, to be honest.

But the blue glow in Summer's eyes flared as if
she knew exactly what I was talking about. 'Oh, yes!
Exactly. And when it all fits together and it works,
and it's like…'

'Like solving a puzzle,' I finished, because clearly
this was what I was doing now. Finishing her fucking sentences.

She smiled, and honest to God, it felt like the sun
coming out. 'Right? I love puzzles.'

That weird feeling in my chest tightened, which,
again, I didn't like. I'd had conversations with the
club girls before, but it was only small talk. They'd
never been interested in what I had to say anyway.
They only wanted my cock.

But there was something about Summer's confession that got to me. She'd said it completely without embarrassment, as if she was comfortable talking to me. As if she thought I'd understand.

Strange, when only a couple of hours before she hadn't been able to get a word out.

'So, you're some kind of genius, right?' I shifted on her, adjusting the way my cock was pressing against her and liking the way she shivered in response.

'Y-yes.' Her nails dug into my shoulder, a flush beginning to creep up her throat.

Oh, I liked that. A lot. 'What's your IQ then?'

'Um…last test I did, over 170.'

Super smart then. Yet, just by shifting my cock, I could make her unable to speak.

Not bad for a dumb fuck.

I grinned and moved again, her breath hissing as I did so. 'Okay, so you actually *are* a genius then.'

'I am.' She arched, her lashes drifting closed. 'Um… Tiger?'

'Yeah?'

'Can you…um…'

'What?' I pushed myself up and back so I could look at her perfect tits. Then I lowered my head, licking one of her hard nipples, loving the way she gasped. 'Am I killing some of those super smart brain cells of yours, baby girl?'

'Yes…oh, *yes.*'

I put my mouth over her nipple and sucked hard, feeling her shudder. Yeah, taking her apart like this was fucking amazing. Addictive even.

'Oh…' she breathed, pressing herself up into my mouth. 'I never thought it would be like this.'

She tasted so sweet and the way she gave a jolt every time I teased her with my tongue was insanely good. I'd never been with a woman who was so sensitive before. I could get used it.

I released her nipple, nuzzling her breast. 'Basically, it's because my IQ is pretty fucking high, too. I'm talking about my sex IQ here.'

'No, I'm serious.' Her blue gaze met mine. 'I thought it would be all really scary, but it wasn't. You made it okay. And you made me feel good. Really, *really* good.'

I didn't know what the hell to say to that, because there was nothing but honesty in her eyes, and it felt kind of…painful. Made me want to wrap her up and protect her, tell her not to make herself so vulnerable. Especially not to me.

'I have to tell you something,' I said. 'You might have thought about me for five years, but I didn't think about you. Not once.' If honesty was what we were going for here, then she had to know. I didn't want her making this into something it wasn't. 'So, if you're thinking that we're—'

'I'm *not* thinking that,' she interrupted, a flash of that temper she hid so well crossing her face. 'That wasn't what I was trying to say. I only wanted to tell you that I think you're amazing. And, well…I *do* like you.'

Again, that honesty. It was a problem. 'Baby,' I said gently. 'You don't know me. And good sex doesn't mean a fucking thing.'

She frowned. 'But I do know you. You carry a gun in the back of your jeans and you love riding that bike. And you used to like teasing me—which, FYI, you still do. Oh, and you're very protective. Also, you have an amazing smile and I used to wish—'

'Everyone knows those things.' I cut her off before she could make me any more uncomfortable than she already was. 'They're not secrets.'

I didn't bother to keep the warning note out of my voice, but apparently she either didn't hear it or simply flat out ignored me, because she gave me a very direct look and said, 'So tell me something no one else knows then.'

Shit. How the hell had I got myself into this situation? There were plenty of things no one else knew about me and I wasn't ashamed of them. That wasn't why I didn't talk about them. I didn't talk about them because they weren't anyone else's business and why she thought they were hers, I had no fucking idea.

You should tell her, dumb fuck. If you're not ashamed, it won't make any difference.

I shook the thought away. Later, I'd tell her later. Right now, my dick was hard and I wanted to suck on her tits some more, then maybe eat her out again, teach her how to ride me just the way I liked.

So I shook my head. 'Later, baby girl. Right now, that hot little pussy of yours is driving me crazy. So how about you just lie there and I'll see if I can cool her down a bit?'

Then I bent my head and took her nipple in my mouth again and tried to ignore the voice in my head that was telling me I was a coward.

CHAPTER ELEVEN

Summer

I DON'T KNOW what time it was when I woke up, but light was streaming through the big windows of Tiger's warehouse apartment, illuminating the vaulted ceiling above me and the heavy beams that criss-crossed it.

I lay on my back staring up at it, for a second disorientated about where I was. But then Tiger shifted beside me, his arm tightening around my waist, and I remembered.

After another intense round of sex on the couch, he'd picked me up and carried me into his bathroom and got in the shower with me. Then he'd washed me carefully, like I was a child, before drying me off and carrying me up to the mezzanine floor where his big low bed was.

He'd done things to me in that bed. Things that had made me scream and cry out his name over and over again. Things I was never going to forget.

I wanted him to do those things all over again, but a quick glance revealed he was still asleep and if

I wanted to have a look around his apartment without him getting in the way, it was going to have to be now.

Carefully I wriggled out from under his arm and slid out of bed, wincing a little at the way some of my muscles decided to remind me of what we'd been getting up to the night before.

It had been worth it, though, *so* worth it.

My clothes were downstairs, so I went down the iron stairs still naked, coming down into the living area. The dark blue T-shirt he'd been wearing the night before was on the floor and on a whim, I picked it up and put it on myself.

It was massive, falling to midthigh, but it was soft and it smelled like him and for some reason I didn't want to take it off.

You don't know me and good sex doesn't mean a fucking thing.

His words from the night before echoed suddenly in my head, making my chest tighten. Which was stupid. Of course I knew it didn't mean a fucking thing and, sure, maybe I didn't know him.

So why do you want to then?

Good question, and one I didn't have an answer to. Perhaps it had been something to do with the sex after all. Or perhaps it was all about the past and my fascination with him. Or maybe it had simply been after I'd gone on and on embarrassingly about how wonderful his tattoo was, and he'd finished my ravings about how everything had fit together by saying it was like a bike engine.

It had been the most perfect simile, the way he'd

understood thrilling me deeply. There weren't many people I could talk to about what excited me, mainly because people's eyes tended to glaze over whenever I mentioned math. But Tiger's hadn't. In one simple sentence, he'd managed to encapsulate my feelings about puzzles and equations, and life in general so perfectly that I knew he'd understood.

Even thinking about it now made a jolt of excitement go through me, making me want to charge right back up the stairs and wake him up, talk to him some more about the similarities between bike engines and mathematics.

Except that wouldn't let me explore and I *really* wanted to do that.

I began to slowly poke around his apartment. It was a massive place, a basic galley kitchen down one end, a motorcycle workshop up the other, with a living area sandwiched in between. Everything was scrupulously clean and tidy, the remotes for the TV and stereo neatly lined up on the coffee table next to a sleek laptop and a stack of bike magazines.

Interesting how he was so tidy, because most guys weren't. Or at least, not the ones I'd had any dealings with.

There were no bookshelves and no books, though. At all. Maybe bikers didn't read? Or were only interested in magazines? There weren't photos or anything either, which was annoying. I'd been hoping to find a few family pics to give me some insights.

Moving past the living area, I wandered over to the workshop end of the space. There was a workbench running along the length of one wall with cupboards and shelves above it, plus a few larger metal cupboards down one end. A big bike was up on a stand, the chrome gleaming in the morning light.

This area too was neat and tidy, the workbench clean except for a shiny piece of metal that looked like it came from the inside of an engine. I picked it up, the weight of it pleasing in my hand, and turned it over, thinking about him, thinking about the tattoo he'd apparently designed himself, the way all those shapes, the spirals and circles and arcs and squares all fit together.

There was more to him than sex and an easy smile, I was sure of it. And I wanted to know what more there was. He was a puzzle and I wanted to solve him.

I turned around to put the piece of metal back down on the workbench, leaning against it, still thinking. Then I suddenly felt heat along my spine, as two large masculine hands came down onto the bench on either side of me.

I went still, shivering as Tiger's tall, rangy body pressed me up against the workbench, his breath feathering the side of my neck. 'Good morning,' he murmured. 'What are you doing down here? You should be upstairs, naked in my bed and ready to suck my cock.'

The feel of him against me and the scent of him, musky and spicy, made my head swim. I sighed, leaning back into him. 'Nothing much. Just looking around.'

'Uh-huh. Stay out of my stuff, baby girl.' His mouth brushed over the nape of my neck, the kiss taking the sting from the words. 'I like you in my shirt, though. You can keep wearing that.' He shifted his hands, sliding them underneath the hem of the T-shirt I wore, cupping my bare butt, squeezing me. 'No panties either. I approve.'

I wanted to arch my hips and press myself into his hands, but I had a feeling that was another distraction technique, like he'd used the night before when he'd avoided telling me something that no one else knew about him.

I turned my head, trying to ignore the feel of his hands on my bare skin. 'Is it later yet?'

'What do you mean later?'

'You were going to tell me something about you that no one else knows.'

He squeezed me again, his hips flexing, and I felt rough denim and heat as he pushed himself against me. 'Yeah, it's not later yet. Not when my dick is hard.'

Definitely distraction techniques. If I wasn't careful, they were going to work, too. Because his fingers were skimming down over the curve of my butt and pressing gently between my thighs from behind, brushing the folds of my sex. And I could feel the pleasure already starting to take hold, the deep, intense throb of it stealing my breath.

But I wasn't going to let him distract me, not this time.

'I'll tell you something that no one knows about me.' I tried to disguise the breathlessness in my voice. 'I...get afraid a lot. In fact, I'm pretty much always afraid.'

His stroking fingers gentled. 'Hate to break it to you, baby girl, but that's not news. I knew you were afraid the moment I met you.'

I could feel my face get hot. I thought I'd hidden it better than that, but obviously I hadn't. 'How did you know?'

'Because you didn't say a word to me. Could barely even look at me. Plus, you seemed to spend a lot of time trying to blend into the background, trying not to be noticed.' His fingers spread out on my butt, then slid up to my hips, holding on to me. 'Seems to me there's a reason for that.'

I swallowed, falling back on my old excuse. 'I don't like people.'

'Yeah, I don't think that's the issue.'

But I didn't want to talk about my dad and the glass house I lived in. It felt too revealing, even more so when I was wearing hardly any clothes. The only reason I'd said it in the first place was to get him to talk.

'You don't want to hear about my pathetic weakness.' I tried to turn around.

But his fingers firmed on my hips, holding me still. 'Fear doesn't make you pathetic, baby. You're only pathetic if you let it stop you from doing what you want to do. And you definitely don't let it stop you. Fuck, you talked your way into the clubhouse in the middle of a goddamn party, even though you were terrified. That's not pathetic. That's gutsy.'

The way he said it, quiet and yet full of conviction, made my throat get tight and a weird prickle start up behind my eyes. Of course I knew I wasn't really as pathetic as I made out. And I didn't need him to tell me that, right?

I opened my mouth to say something, I don't even know what, but he was still talking in the same quiet tone. 'And if you've got the guts to do that… Okay, you want to know something about me that no one else knows? I can't fucking read.'

Shock pulsed through me and I was turning around before I could think better of it.

He'd loosened his grip on me and had taken a step back, standing there staring down at me with those dark amber eyes. He was only wearing a pair of half-buttoned jeans, leaving a whole lot of gorgeous sculpted muscle and dark ink on show. He casually put his hands in his pockets, his posture loose and easy, but there was a guarded expression on his face.

'You can't read?' I echoed stupidly.

'No. Always had difficulty with it when I was at school and then I had to leave and…' He lifted one of those powerful shoulders. 'I never learned.'

I couldn't believe it. He was so strong, so sure of himself. So confident and yet for some reason he'd never developed one of life's most basic skills. 'Why not?'

Something crossed his face, gone too fast before I could see what it was. 'Like I said, I could never get the hang of it at school. Not that I was at school a lot anyway.'

'But how come? Why weren't you in school? Surely you had someone who could teach you how to—'

'My mom was a whore.' The words were sharp,

cutting me off. 'She took johns during the day because she didn't like doing it at night, and she needed
me to look after my kid brother. So I did. And when
I got older, she needed me to look after her as well,
because some of those johns were violent fucks who
had no respect.' Something dark and metallic glit-
tered in his gaze, not the bright gold of arousal but
what looked like a sullen kind of anger. 'She left
when I was sixteen and took Tommy with her, and
then it was too late to go back to school, so I didn't.
Joined the Knights instead. Don't need to fucking
read to be a brother.'

I blinked at him, trying to take all this in. His
childhood sounded…awful. Worse than mine by a
long shot. 'Your mom was a…p-prostitute?'

'Yeah.' The anger in his gaze burned a little
brighter. 'You got a problem with that? She had to
feed me and Tommy somehow and that was the only
way she could do it.'

'No, no problem,' I said quickly. 'But she left
you? At sixteen?' There was something painful in
my chest, a terrible sympathy, because I knew what
it was like to have a mother leave you. I knew the
hole that it left, even though I tried not to think about
it too often.

Unexpectedly he looked away, but not before I
caught the flash of pain that glinted in his eyes. 'She
had to go. I don't blame her for leaving.'

'But you were sixteen. That's so young. Why did
she go?'

Another shrug, as if he didn't care. 'I don't know.'

I blinked again. 'You don't know?'

'She didn't fucking tell me, okay?' His rough voice had got sharper, harder, the anger in his eyes bleeding into his words. 'One day I got home and she and Tommy weren't there. She'd just…gone.'

The painful feeling in my chest ached. At least my mom had kissed me goodbye before she'd left. Told me to be a good girl for my dad and that one day she'd come back for me. She never had of course, but that was a whole other story. At least I knew why she'd gone—because living with Dad had become impossible for her.

'I'm so sorry.' It was trite, but I didn't know what else to say. 'That must have been awful.'

'You don't need to be fucking sorry.' Tension had crept into his posture, his shoulders going tight. 'Got nothing to do with you.'

'I know that, but I know what it's like to have a parent walk out on you. My mom did when I was little. She always told me she'd come back, but…' I stopped. I didn't want to make this about me. This was about him. About the fact that he'd been left alone at sixteen years old. God.

'Parents,' he said, as if that explained everything, his mouth twisting into a mirthless smile. 'What are you gonna do?'

It sounded flippant, but I knew it wasn't. I could see the anger there, glowing beneath the smile he was trying to cover it with. 'What about your dad? Do you have any other relatives?'

'No. Never knew who my dad was and never wanted to find out.' He rolled his shoulders like he was trying to get rid of the tension in them. 'The Knights are all the family I need.'

'Do they know you can't read?'

''Course not. Why do you think I said it was something no one else knew?'

'But why didn't you learn?' I couldn't seem to leave the subject alone. 'I mean, how do you do anything? Do you get people to read to you or what?'

'Technology, baby. It's a wonderful thing.' He took his hands out of his pockets and stalked towards me again, slow and fluid, tiger by name, tiger by nature. 'I got a phone that reads shit out to me and I can dictate texts. Same with my computer. And I don't need to read to be able to put an engine together.'

He closed the distance between us, backing me up against the workbench and pinning me there with his body, his hands coming down on either side of me once again. He was hard, I could feel him pressing against me, could see the glint of arousal in his eyes. But that anger was still there, too, and it was glowing hot.

He might act like he didn't care about his mother leaving, or about not being able to read, but he did.

'Why did you tell me?' I ignored the hard ridge that was nudging between my thighs, looking up into his strong, fierce face.

'You wanted to know. So I told you.'

'But you haven't told anyone else.'

'No, because it's a fucking depressing subject.' He nudged me a little more firmly and a hot burst of sensation flooded through me. 'Don't go thinking this makes you special, baby girl. I don't care who knows.'

Oh, yes, he did. Why else would I be the only one? It hurt that I wasn't special to him, because he was special to me, but still…he'd told me all the same. He'd given this secret to me and no matter what he said, it *did* feel special to me.

I lifted my hands to his face, obeying some instinct that told me that touch was the way to connect with him, the prickle of his morning beard against my palms a delicious roughness. 'I think you do care,' I said calmly. 'So why don't you let me teach you?'

CHAPTER TWELVE

Tiger

SUMMER'S BLUE EYES had that serious look in them again, and she'd taken my face between her palms. And for some reason I could feel that touch settle down through me like I'd popped a Valium or something. It made me feel warm, made the tension in my shoulders and neck release.

Crazy. I wanted to lift her up and fuck her right here on the workbench, not fall in a damn puddle at her feet.

I should never have said anything. I didn't know why I had. Just…her confession about being afraid had hit me hard and I hadn't been able to let it go. For some insane fucking reason, I wanted to give her something back and so the words had come out, like I'd been waiting to say them for goddamn years. Then I'd poured out the shit about Mom and Tommy, too, and the mistake had got worse and worse.

Now she was looking at me like I was a lost puppy she wanted to take home with her and I didn't like how that made my heart kick hard in my chest. This

girl wasn't looking for a cock to ride. She was looking at *me*.

It made me feel naked. Like walking into a rival
MC's clubhouse without my cut.

I didn't like that. Because, really, who the fuck
liked being vulnerable? I didn't. It reminded me of
getting home that day when I was sixteen, and coming inside to find it empty. I'd thought Mom had
taken Tommy out to the park, so I hadn't worried.
But then it had got dark and she still hadn't turned
up. I'd gone out searching for her and couldn't find
her, and had started to get worried. It wasn't until I'd
come home again and gone up into her bedroom that
I saw the empty closet. And the dresser top that used
to have all her perfumes and shit on it wiped clean.

I'd never forget that feeling. My stomach had
dropped away and I'd thought I was going to be sick.
I'd gone into Tommy's room to see what was going
on there, but all his clothes were gone, too. And so
was the stuffed bear he took with him everywhere.

That was when I knew for certain.

They were gone and they weren't coming back.

So, no. I didn't want to feel like that ever again.

'I don't need you to teach me.' I couldn't keep
the edge from my voice. 'I'm happy with things the
way they are.'

*What about the letters, dumb fuck? Don't you
want to know what's in them?*

No. Those letters could stay unread until fucking
Doomsday as far as I was concerned.

'I don't think you are.' She was so goddamn serious. 'Why won't you let me help?'

''Cause I don't want your help. I didn't bring you here to teach me to read, I brought you here so I could fuck you, end of story.'

She frowned, temper shifting in her eyes. 'Why do you say stuff like that? Why do you make it sound like nothing?'

I opened my mouth to tell her that was because it *was* nothing, no matter what she thought. But then I felt my phone buzz in my pocket.

I held up a hand and pulled away from her, grabbing the phone and looking down to see Smoke's picture on the screen. Fuck. What was he calling about?

I turned away from Summer and hit the answer button. 'What?'

'Keep's getting antsy about the chief's daughter,' Smoke said, getting straight to the point. 'And he thinks you're either hiding something or letting yourself get distracted.'

Jesus, this was all I needed. 'Am I the only fucking brother in the MC?' I didn't bother hiding my temper. 'Why's he fucking on me about it?'

'I dunno, man. You protected her once and have a connection with her?'

'You're with Cat and she was once her sister-in-law. Why don't you find her?'

'Hey, chill the fuck out.' Smoke sounded as pissed as I felt. 'What's your problem?'

I took a breath, trying to get a handle on myself. Because I knew what the problem was. That little girl behind me asking me questions I didn't want to answer and telling me things I didn't want to hear.

Not to mention Keep being on my butt about finding her and taking her in.

And I didn't want to do that. I hadn't finished with her.

Apart from all the serious fucking I was planning on doing, I hadn't discovered anything about why she was so afraid all the time or why she'd run from her father in the first place, and I wasn't going to let her go anywhere near Keep until I'd found those things out.

Sure, she was asking me about uncomfortable shit, but I could deal. I wasn't a pussy-ass bitch. It had been years since Mom left and I had a whole new family now. A family that had my back and wouldn't ever leave.

She could help you out with those letters.

Ah, fuck the letters. I didn't want to read them even if I could.

They'd started arriving about a year after Mom left and I knew what my own name looked like; they were addressed to me. The handwriting was familiar, too. I knew they were from Mom.

When the first one had arrived, I'd carried it around with me for weeks, wanting to know what it said and yet so angry I could hardly deal. I could have asked someone to read it for me, but that would have meant giving away the fact that I couldn't, and at the time I hadn't been able to stand the fact that someone would know.

I'd nearly thrown that letter away a thousand times, but something wouldn't let me. In the end, I'd stuffed it in a box and forgotten about it. Same thing happened a year later, I got another letter. Then another. And pretty soon I had a little pile of letters all from Mom, all of which I couldn't read. Which she knew.

I don't know why I kept them, but I still had 'em all in a drawer upstairs. Waiting for the day that I'd rip them open and read them. But that day hadn't come.

'There's no problem,' I growled to Smoke. 'I've got more important things to handle right now.'

'What? That girl you took home last night? Didn't mention her to Keep, by the way. Thought he didn't need to know.'

Well, that was something. 'Thanks, man,' I said grudgingly. 'So am I gonna get him riding my butt this morning about it or what?'

'Leave him to me. I'll deal with it.'

Smoke was Keep's nephew and had a different kind of relationship with him than the rest of us. The prez was a fucking hard-ass, but Smoke seemed to know how to handle him and I appreciated my buddy putting his neck out for me.

But that was the thing about the club. We had each other's backs and in the shitshow that was life, that was the most important thing in it.

'I fucking owe you,' I muttered.

'Yeah, you do.' There was a pause. 'That girl one of the important things to do?'

What I should have said was 'What girl?' But I didn't. Instead I nearly said 'Yeah' without thinking about it. A mistake. Especially when it came to club business, because *nothing* was more important than club business to me.

'No,' I lied, conscious of Summer standing behind me, watching me. I knew she was watching me because I could feel her gaze boring into my back.

'Yeah, sure,' Smoke said, like he knew exactly how big a liar I was. 'I've got one of my own at home, remember?'

I scowled. 'It's not like that.'

'The fuck it isn't.' The prick sounded amused.

Still scowling, I disconnected the call without a response, which would probably give me away as much as more denial would, but I didn't care. I didn't want to keep talking about the subject.

'Well?' Summer asked quietly. 'You didn't answer my question.'

I flung the phone over onto the coffee table, then turned around.

It made no sense why the sight of her with all that pretty white-gold hair down around her shoulders or the fact that she was wearing nothing but my T-shirt should get me harder than steel, but it did and suddenly I didn't give a shit about anything. Not about those letters, not about the fact I'd told her something not even Smoke, my best buddy, knew. And not about the fact that for some inexplicable reason she wanted to help me.

All that stuff was bullshit.

Feeling good, that was the point of everything, wasn't it? Because life was short and shitty, so you grabbed the good times while you could.

'Come here,' I said.

She didn't hesitate, coming to stand right in front of me. There was a crease between her fair brows, her gaze searching mine. 'Are you okay?'

'I will be once my cock is in your mouth.'

Her eyes narrowed and I had the weird feeling that she saw right through me.

Then she said, 'Don't think I don't know distraction techniques when I see them.'

Shit.

I forced a smile. 'You make me come, then maybe we'll talk after.'

'Is that a promise?'

'Depends on how quickly you make me come.'

Her lips pursed and she fixed me with that stern look she did so well. 'You know I'm going to hold you to that.'

Christ, this little girl challenging me all the fucking time. I shook my head. 'Aren't you supposed to be scared of me? Maybe you'd better stop ordering me around.'

Her mouth twitched and I found myself staring at it, already imagining it wrapped around my cock. 'Apparently I'm not *that* scared of you any more.'

'It's my dick. It's magic.'

She laughed. 'So, do I get to see this magic dick of yours then? Or are you going to keep talking?'

This was a side of her I hadn't seen before, a glimpse of the spirit that lurked underneath her fear. Fuck, it was sexy. 'You're very forward for a virgin, you know that?'

'But I'm not a virgin. Not any more.'

'Thank fuck. On your knees, baby girl.'

She didn't even blink, doing exactly what I told her and graceful as hell with it. Then she looked up at me from her position on the floor, all big eyes and white-blonde hair and innocence, and I was suddenly hard enough to hammer nails.

'You'll have to tell me what to do,' she said, all seriousness now. 'This is another first time for me.'

It would be the gentlemanly thing to do. But then, there was nothing gentlemanly about me. And besides, I actually didn't want to tell her. I wanted her to find out what I liked on her own, because she was interested. Because she wanted to explore me, discover me. *Me.* Not some random guy.

It was stupid. 'Take me deep and suck me hard.' That's what I should have said to her. Yet what came out instead was 'Use your imagination.'

A fleeting look of worry crossed her face. 'I know, but you must be used to women who can do it really well, and I'm hardly in that league. You might not enjoy it.'

Jesus, her honesty. It got to me. The fact it mattered to her that I enjoy it. I mean, sure, the club girls were good and wore that skill like a badge of honour. It mattered to them, too, but for different reasons. Reasons that were more about them and their status than they were about pleasing me personally.

I reached down and cupped Summer's cheek. Her skin was so soft it ought to have been illegal. I was sure my hand with all the calluses and scars I'd got from fixing engines would scrape her. Yet if it did, she didn't seem to care, leaning into my palm like a little cat, her gaze on mine.

My chest went tight and I almost forgot what I'd been going to say. 'Whatever you do, I'll enjoy it,' I forced out, wanting her to know this because it felt important. 'Fuck, I already can hardly speak.'

She flushed and her lashes dropped, her gaze on my dick, which was currently pushing so hard against my zipper it was amazing the thing didn't unzip itself.

Her hand lifted and she put out a finger, tracing my cock through the denim, a slow up and down that made my breath catch. Very similar to the way I'd touched her pussy the night before, come to think of it...

Oh, fuck. This was payback, wasn't it?

'Don't be shy,' I muttered. Hell, was that really my voice? All husky and rough? 'Get my dick out.'

'Wait. I'm just figuring it out.' She kept on touching me, slowly and experimentally, finding the head of my cock and rubbing gently over the top, making my breath hiss in my throat.

Yeah, I liked it hard and fast, not this slow kind of bullshit. But the careful way she was touching me and the look of concentration on her face, as if this was really important to her...somehow I couldn't bring myself to tell her to stop.

'You want to play with me?' I asked hoarsely. 'Is that what you're doing?'

She shot me a wide blue glance. 'Is that okay? I mean, you wanted me to figure it out, so I'd like to try.'

'Sure.' I'd kept my hand where it was on her cheek and couldn't resist stroking her with my thumb. 'You just might kill me is all.'

She flushed again with pleasure. 'Well, you killed me last night so maybe it's my turn.'

And she *was* fucking killing me. Slowly and by inches as she fumbled around with my zipper, then tugged it down. I hadn't bothered with underwear when I'd got up, so the moment she got my jeans open, my dick was right in her face.

Her eyes went wide, which was incredibly satisfying, and I found myself sliding my hand to the back of her neck and gripping on tight. Not forcing her forward, just holding on. I couldn't drag my gaze from what she was doing. She put her hand on me, her fingers stroking my cock, exploring it like she'd never seen anything like it before in her life.

It was the hottest fucking thing.

My pulse was racing, my heart rate through the roof. And she was just touching me. That's all she was doing, just stroking me. Christ, I hadn't been kidding when I'd told her she was going to kill me. She would. Literally.

Then she finally gripped me, curving those pale fingers around the base of my dick, squeezing me. And she looked up into my face as she did so, obviously wanting to see my response.

'I'm not fragile, baby girl,' I muttered. 'You can do that harder.'

So she did, squeezing me harder, and I couldn't stop myself. I held on to the back of her neck with one hand while I lifted the other and covered her fingers where they gripped me, then I showed her how to pump me.

God, it felt good. The warmth of her hand and the

pressure. The expression of fierce concentration on her face. It was probably the same expression she got when she was figuring out a math problem, which shouldn't have been sexy but was all the same.

She was a fast learner, though, and soon I didn't have to show her what to do, she had it all figured out without any problems. My hand dropped from hers as she began to find a rhythm, varying the strokes and the pressure. Then she stopped a couple of times, circling the head of my aching dick with her thumb and then slicking across the top of it.

Holy shit, she made me feel so good it was insane. She wasn't practised at all, but the way she approached it, like she was going to work at this until she got it right, was hot as fuck.

'Yeah.' I was fucking babbling now. 'So good, baby girl. That's right. You keep doing that, you're gonna make me come so hard.'

She leaned forward and licked me, and I almost lost it. Almost fucking came there and then. Her tongue was like a blowtorch, setting me on fire, and there was only one way this was going to end.

I thrust both hands into her hair and held on, pushing my aching dick between those pretty pink lips before she could pull away, feeling the heat of her mouth surround me. She made a little sound, kind of like a groan, and her hands came out to grip my thighs, holding on tight.

'You okay?' I demanded hoarsely, feeling the shakes beginning already and wanting to thrust deep into her throat, but holding back because I didn't want to lay it on her all at once.

She gave a nod, so I began to ease deeper, my breathing harsh in the silence of the room, every sense I had centred on the heat of that mouth of hers and the incredible pleasure it was giving me.

I nudged the back of her throat and she tensed, so I pulled back, giving her a moment before thrusting in again. Her nails dug hard into my thighs and she gave a groan that sounded hungry, so I began to move faster, harder.

Her hair in my hands was so silky and warm that I gripped it tighter, pulling her head back a little so I could look down into her face, so I could see my dick sliding in between those perfect lips.

So fucking hot.

Her blue eyes met mine and I could see the hunger in them and the glaze of pleasure, and it was like an extra kick to know she was getting off on this as much as I was.

I'd got head from so many women and it had always been good. But this… Holy hell, I don't know what it was, but what she was doing eclipsed every single blow job I'd ever had.

'Gonna go harder,' I warned her. 'You okay?'

She gave a frantic nod so I went ahead and upped the pace, and it was so goddamn good. Her gaze was trained on mine as if I was the only thing she could see and that lit me up, too, made me feel like a fucking god.

'You're gonna make me come.' I looked down into those incredible blue eyes. 'Oh, baby girl, you're gonna make me come so fucking hard.'

I could feel the orgasm building at the base of my

spine, the tension winding tighter and tighter. I was going faster now, fucking her mouth without mercy, and she took it all, gripping onto me so tight it was a wonder she didn't draw blood.

Then she did something with her tongue—I don't know what the fuck it was—and maybe it was the sheer unexpectedness of it that got me but it made lightning shoot straight down my spine to my cock, and that was it, I was gone.

'Take it all,' I groaned. 'Fucking take everything I give you.'

And she did.

And when the orgasm crushed me into fucking dust and I came down the back of her throat, all I could see were her eyes, blue as the sky.

Making me feel as if I were flying.

CHAPTER THIRTEEN

Summer

WATCHING TIGER COME and knowing I was the one who'd done it to him had to rank as one of the hottest things I'd ever seen. And the most powerful.

It was weird how I was on my knees in front of him, supposedly at a disadvantage, and yet he was the one who'd come completely undone.

His cock was pulsing in my mouth and I could taste him, salty and thick. His head was thrown back, the tendons of his throat standing out rigidly as he gasped, the sound of my name echoing around us.

His fingers were wound in my hair and it was a little painful, but I barely felt it. I was too busy looking at him, watching what I'd done to him and feeling the same rush I got when I solved a complex equation.

I'd done this to him. This experienced, jaded biker was shaking and all because I'd taken him in my mouth and sucked him hard.

He'd had to take over in the end, but I didn't count that as a failure. I'd filed away what he'd shown me, remembered it so that next time I could fully take charge.

If there is a next time.

I shook the thought away. Of course there'd be a next time. Maybe later, after we'd had the talk he'd promised me. I knew more about what he liked now. I could use that knowledge and maybe it wouldn't be him seducing me. Maybe it would be me seducing him.

The idea sent a thrill down my spine, making me shiver, making the ache between my thighs more intense.

His grip in my hair loosened and slowly he pulled out of my mouth, tucking himself away. His hands shook as he did so and that gave me a thrill, too.

Hell, everything about him gave me a thrill.

Once he'd zipped himself back up, I leaned forward and rested my cheek against the warm skin of his stomach, feeling the rock-hard muscles of his abs tense and flex. His hands returned to my hair, combing through it, then massaging my scalp with firm, circular movements of his fingers.

It felt so good that I closed my eyes, enjoying his touch and the heat of his body, the scent of musk and spice that was all Tiger. But pretty soon I wanted those massaging fingers to touch me elsewhere and so I had to move.

Because I wasn't going to let him distract me again. That was exactly what he'd done with his blow job demands and we both knew it. He didn't want to talk about his mother, or about the fact that I'd offered to teach him to read, and, hell, I couldn't blame him. He was such a tough, strong guy and he must hate having his vulnerabilities exposed.

But I wanted to help him. I'd hated the look of pain in his eyes when he'd told me about his mother's disappearance and I wanted to make it better for him. Because I'd bet the entire, meagre contents of my bank account that he didn't have anyone else who wanted to help him the way I wanted to help him.

It was probably a good time to start asking myself why this was so important to me, but I decided I didn't want to answer that question right now. It was enough that I wanted to. Anyway, he'd brought me here and hidden me from Keep and from my dad, so helping him seemed the right thing to do.

After a moment of silence, I felt Tiger move, bending to lift me up into his arms, and I let him, loving his strength and the feeling of lying against his warm, bare chest. Loving how he held me as if I was made of glass and he had to be careful of me, gentle with me.

It made me feel special, which was a dangerous thing to feel, but I couldn't help it. I wanted to feel special to someone, since I'd never really been special to anyone, and this was as close as I was going to get.

I leaned my head against his shoulder and looked up at him. His golden eyes gleamed as they met mine and there was a very satisfied expression on his face. 'Did I do okay?' My voice was hoarse, probably due to him pressing against the back of my throat, and it felt a little raw.

'Do I really need to answer that?' He headed towards the armchair opposite the couch. 'You made me go fucking blind.'

'Oh.' There was a warm glow in the centre of my chest and I smiled, pleased with myself. 'You did have to show me what to do at the end, but next time I promise I'll do better.'

'If you do any better, you'll fucking kill me.' He sat down in the armchair and arranged me across his lap, keeping one arm around me so I could lie back against his shoulder, while with the other he toyed with the hem of the T-shirt I wore. 'I'm planning on some payback already.'

I shivered again at the heat in his voice. 'I'm sure you are. But that's not what we're doing now.'

'Oh?' One dark brow rose. 'And what exactly are we doing now?'

'What you promised. You told me if I made you come, we'd talk.'

He gazed at me from underneath this long, thick black lashes, dark amber gleaming. 'That was a dumb thing to say, wasn't it?'

'You were the one who said it.'

'Hmm.' His fingers stroked my bare knee. 'Fine, let's talk. Tell me why you're afraid all the time.'

I blinked, trying to ignore the light touch of his fingers on my bare skin and only just stopping myself from pulling a face. Talking about myself wasn't exactly what I'd planned. 'I don't know,' I said vaguely. 'It's just… I've always felt afraid of things.'

'Yeah, and that's not a fucking answer. Perhaps it'll become clearer if I do this.' His fingers slid higher, up the inside of my thigh.

I frowned at him. 'What did I say about distraction techniques?'

'Then answer my question.'

I sighed and looked down, raising a hand to trace his beautiful tattoos. I could see the tiger on his right arm, all strength and grace and ferocity. 'Did you design this one, too?' I touched the tiger's gleaming fangs that seemed to close around his shoulder.

'No. Got that when I patched in and the tattoo guy did it for me. Now you're being distracting.' His finger caught me under my chin and tipped my head back so I met his gaze. 'Come on, baby girl. Talk to me.'

'I don't know,' I said quietly. 'Maybe it was growing up in a house that feels like it's going to collapse at any second if you make a wrong move.'

'Why did it feel like that?'

'Oh, Dad. His moods. You never knew where you stood with him and you never knew what could set him off. He used to shout at me for no reason, and I hated it so I tried to keep out of his way as much as possible.' I swallowed, a familiar tense, anxious feeling gripping me. 'And my brother used to do the same thing.'

Tiger's dark brows drew down in a sudden, ferocious frown. Maybe that should have scared me, too, the way it always had whenever Dad had looked at me that way, but it didn't. Because this was Tiger, and sitting here in his arms I'd never felt safer in my entire life. 'Your brother. My buddy's old lady used to go out with him and he used to hurt her. He ever do that to you?'

I hadn't had much to do with Cat when she'd been with Justin so I didn't really know her. 'No, he didn't. I kept out of his way, the same way I kept out of Dad's.'

But Tiger's frown didn't lift. 'He fucking better not have laid a finger on you, get me? Because I'll kill him if he did.'

At first I thought Tiger was joking, but he wasn't smiling. Shit, he really would, wouldn't he?

I wrapped my fingers around his wrist. 'Don't kill my brother, Tiger. Please.'

He grunted, but the feral look in his eyes didn't waver. 'Just a warning.'

'Look, Dad and Justin didn't hurt me, so I'm not sure why I was even so scared.' Now I'd said it out loud, it all seemed so stupid. A lifetime of fear just because I didn't like my daddy shouting at me? How pathetic. 'They never did anything to me.'

'Fear doesn't come from nowhere, baby,' Tiger said fiercely. 'And being an abusive fuck doesn't necessarily mean punching the shit out of someone. Making you feel bad about yourself, making you feel scared, that's all abusive shit right there, and you know what? At least if someone hits you that's honest. At least you know where you stand. But with that kind of emotional bullshit, it's hard. You have no comeback and no way to protect yourself.'

I stared at him, suddenly thinking about all the things that Dad had said to me over the years, the jabs and criticisms, the subtle way he used my fear against me. 'He told me Mom left because of me,' I said hoarsely, not even realising I was going to mention it until the words came out. 'He said that I'd made him angry and that Mom didn't like it when he was angry and so she'd gone.' There was a lump in my throat and it felt tight and sore. I tried to turn my head away, feeling vulnerable and wishing I'd never spoken, but Tiger's grip on my chin tightened, holding me so I couldn't.

'Go on,' he growled.

I didn't want to, but there was something about his hot amber gaze on mine that felt reassuring. Even though it burned with anger, I knew the anger wasn't directed at me. It was for me. And I liked that. No one had ever been angry on my behalf before.

'He said that if I wanted her to come back,' I went on, even though it was painful to say it out loud, 'if I ever wanted to see her again, I'd better be a good girl and not make him mad.' I swallowed. 'I shouldn't have believed him. I don't know why I did. At the time I felt bewildered because I didn't know what I'd done to make him angry. All I knew was that I had to make up for it somehow, so I tried to be as good as I could be. And eventually I thought that if I made myself invisible, he wouldn't see me and if he couldn't see me, I wouldn't make him angry. And then maybe Mom would come home. It's stupid now I think about it, because how could Mom know if he was angry or not when she wasn't there? Anyway, I don't know why he said those things to me. Maybe he was simply angry about Mom leaving and didn't know what to do—'

Tiger's grip tightened, cutting me off. 'Don't excuse him,' he said, his voice hard. 'That was a terrible thing to say to you. No father worth the name blames his little girl for his own fuck-ups, no matter how goddamn angry he is.'

'It's okay,' I croaked, not wanting to make a fuss about it. 'Look, the whole being scared thing was my fault anyway. I'm kind of pathetic and emotional and—'

But Tiger cut me off again, sharp and hard. 'Is that what he told you?'

'No, of course not. But I know that I am and I—'

'It's *not* your fucking fault your mom left. Why do you still believe him? Why are you taking the blame?'

I stared at him, stunned. 'I'm not!'

'Yes, you are.' There was a fierce, angry light in his eyes. 'You're excusing him. You're saying you're pathetic and you're not. You're just fucking not. You're steel, baby. Coming down to the club-house, shoving Crash when he put the moves on you. Getting all up in my grille. Fuck, you wanna know how many people challenge me the way you did? Not one. No one would fucking dare.'

The way he said the words and the conviction in his voice did things to me. I hadn't thought I still blamed myself for the way Mom left. I *knew* it had simply been Dad's anger talking, but...

Realisation began to settle down inside me, and with it came pain. Because all my life my father had made me feel small and weak, and I'd *let* him.

Even when I told myself I hadn't believed the things he'd said all those years ago, there was still a small part of me that did.

A tear slid down my cheek and I didn't bother to wipe it away. 'Mom kissed me goodbye when she left. She said she'd see me again. Dad was always so angry afterwards, no matter how good I was. I wondered if I wasn't being good enough and some-how…she knew and…stayed away.'

The fierce light in Tiger's eyes didn't fade, yet somehow it became warmer. He'd kept that big, rough hand on my cheek, and now he brushed the tear away with his thumb, a gentle movement that pierced my heart straight through. 'You didn't drive her away, Summer,' he said, and that warmth was in his rough voice, too, wrapping me up like a velvet blanket. 'And you didn't keep her away either. Your father's an asshole for telling you that. I bet she left because she couldn't stand his shit, but honestly? She should never have left you behind in the first place. She should have come back. She should have fought like a fucking demon to get you.'

I felt every one of those words hit me like sparks thrown from a fire. And they touched something cold in my heart that I hadn't known existed, ignit-ing a warmth that hadn't been there before, thawing everything icy inside me.

Another tear slipped out, though I tried not to let it. 'We were supposed to be talking about you. Not me.'

'I prefer talking about you.' His thumb moved, brushing away a tear again. 'Don't let your dad af-fect how you feel about yourself, baby girl. The only power he has over you is the power you give him, so don't give it to him. And you can do that. You're stronger than you think. Jesus, if you can face down an MC enforcer like me, you can face down anyone.'

He was right. I knew it deep in my bones. Maybe the knowledge had always been there and I hadn't wanted to face it, because the thought of confronting my dad was scary. And not because of what he might do to me, but because of the way he could hurt me inside.

But Tiger seemed to see deeper into me than I saw myself. And if he thought I was strong, then maybe I actually was. He wasn't a guy who would lie or blow smoke. He didn't manipulate people. He told the truth.

I gave him a watery smile, leaning into the comfort of his palm against my skin. 'You're not that scary.'

'I'm pretty fucking tough.'

'Not as tough as you make out.' I put my hand over his where it rested on my cheek. 'Your mother didn't come back for you either, did she?'

His gaze flickered as I hit a nerve he didn't want touched. But I didn't look away and I kept my hand over his. I wanted him to know he could talk to me about that, that he could trust me. 'It's not the same,' he muttered eventually.

'Why not?'

'Your mom said goodbye to you.'

'So? Clearly that didn't stop me from blaming myself.'

'I don't blame myself.'

But he did, that was obvious. 'Tiger…'

He looked away. 'Come on, I'll make you breakfast. But don't forget I owe you one.'

'You owe me one what?'

'One orgasm.' His hold shifted and I found myself sliding off his lap and onto my feet.

Yeah, he really did *not* want to talk about his mother and I couldn't help the sharp spike of disappointment that slid under my skin. I'd laid myself open for him yet he wouldn't give me any of himself? It didn't seem fair.

He got to his feet and then, unexpectedly, reached for my hand and threaded his fingers through mine. His amber gaze was suddenly direct. 'I'll talk while I cook, okay?'

CHAPTER FOURTEEN

Tiger

TALKING TO SUMMER about my shitty past was something I definitely didn't want to do. But she'd looked so hurt that I couldn't seem to stop myself. If she wanted to hear it, then where would be the harm in telling her?

It was all in the past now anyway. It didn't have any fucking power over me.

I got Summer to sit on the stool at the counter that divided the rest of my space from the kitchen, while I opened the fridge and got out some eggs and bacon.

If she wanted to hear this shit, then I'd tell her while I cooked, give me something else to focus on. Of course I'd rather have given her the orgasm I owed her, but she clearly wasn't going to drop this until I'd given it to her.

You want to tell her, come on.

Well, okay, maybe I did. She'd been upfront with me about her asshole of a father and how he'd basically undermined her confidence, making her think she was to blame for her mother leaving. Making her scared of him.

It made me want to punch that fucker in the face so hard it was a good thing Summer was here to distract me with my own issues. Because I was definitely itching to get on my bike, take a trip down to the station and confront that asshole. Not a good idea, what with him being the police chief and all.

Trying to ignore the urge towards violence, I put some coffee in the coffee maker, then got a pan prepared for the eggs and bacon. I could feel her staring at my back, waiting for me to speak, and since this wasn't going to get any easier, plus the fact that I wasn't a fucking pussy, I just came out with it. 'No, Mom never came back for me. I never knew why she left. One day she was there, the next she was gone.'

'Did you…try to find her?'

'Yeah, but I was only sixteen. I wanted to go to the cops, see if they could find her, but I'd got a name for myself by that stage and I didn't want to draw attention. Plus…' I grimaced as I cracked the eggs into the pan. 'Mom was a whore. The cops don't want to involve themselves with that if they don't have to.'

'No, I understand,' she said quietly. 'So what did you do?'

'I'd already started prospecting for the Knights so they took me in, helped me out. Looked out for me. They became my family.'

'Do they know about the reading thing?'

I slapped some bacon down beside the eggs. 'No. Smoke's maybe guessed, but we've never talked about it. I can write my own name and sign shit, so that's not a problem. I can dictate texts on my phone and it reads them out to me, plus I can do the same with emails on the laptop. I've got a system worked out so it's fine.'

'But you never wanted to learn? Not once?'

I stared at the cooking food, pushing it around with a fork. I'd always told myself it didn't matter that I couldn't read. Sure, it was fucking annoying sometimes, but I'd managed to get through life without so far. Why bother learning when I was fine?

You know why you haven't learned.

'About a year after Mom left, I got a letter.' The words were out before I could stop them, and now they were out, there was nothing for it but to go on. 'It was addressed to me and I recognised the handwriting. It was from Mom. She'd tried when I was younger to teach me a few basics of the alphabet so I could recognise a few things, like my name and stuff. But I couldn't read a whole letter and she knew that.'

Behind me there was silence.

I pushed around the bacon again, watching it sizzle. Fuck. This was harder than I'd expected. 'I wanted to throw the fucking thing away, tear it up, but I didn't. I carried it around with me for months. I thought about getting someone to read it to me, but that would mean admitting I couldn't read it. Also I just…'

'You were angry at her.' Summer's voice was soft.

She's not wrong.

I gritted my teeth. Yeah, okay. Maybe I was. 'The next year I got another one and then another. I kept getting them. So now I've got this pile of letters upstairs and I still haven't read a fucking word.'

There was another long silence.

I flipped over the eggs and made sure the bacon didn't burn, trying not to think about those goddamn letters and how much I didn't want to know what was in them.

Because you don't want to know why she left in case it was *your fault.*

It wasn't my fault. I hadn't done a goddamn thing. *She* was the one who'd left *me*. Without a fucking word. Not even bothering to tell me where she was going and taking Tommy with her, too.

I used to tell myself I didn't care, that it didn't touch me. But of course it had. I'd never forgiven her, not after everything I'd tried to do for her. Protecting her from the pricks that would have hurt her, getting some part-time work under the table and giving her the cash for when things were tight, looking after Tommy so she could work…

Then she'd left. Thanks for nothing, Tiger.

The food was ready so I slid the eggs and bacon onto some plates and carried one over to her, getting out a knife and fork for her, too.

She gave me a quick glance as I put the silverware down before glancing down at her plate. 'This looks delicious. I could read them for you, if you like.'

She said the last sentence in exactly the same tone as the first and I almost missed it. Then I heard. And I had to turn away, going for the coffee maker, because I didn't know what the fuck to say.

Okay, that was a lie. I knew.

'No.' I pulled out a couple of mugs from the shelf. 'I don't want to know.'

Another silence.

Then she said, 'I didn't think you were a coward, Tiger.'

I snapped my head around, a surge of anger going through me, and met her blue eyes. They were clear and direct, and didn't flinch away even though I must have been snarling. 'No one calls me a fucking coward,' I growled. 'No one.'

Her chin lifted a little. 'Then why haven't you got someone to read them to you?'

'Because I don't need to know what the fuck is in them.'

'Bullshit,' she said sternly. 'I think you do. I think you're desperate to know. But you're afraid of what you might find.'

'I'm not—'

'You're afraid you're to blame, aren't you?'

I don't know how she saw through me, right the way through to my goddamn shrivelled-up excuse for a soul, but she did. And this time I was the one who had to turn away, using making the coffee as an excuse not to have to deal with the look in her eyes.

'I know what it's like, Tiger,' she went on, clearly not picking up on my 'shut the hell up' vibes. 'I know what it's like to blame yourself. I mean, wasn't that what you told me about my own mother just now?'

I stalked over to the fridge for some cream. 'It's not the same.'

'You said that already. But it is. We both had people leave us and we both don't know why. God, at least your mother reached out to you. I would have given anything for a letter from mine.'

The wistfulness in her voice hit me like a hammer to the back of the head, making me stop dead.

You tool. Sulking over some fucking letters. She's right. You're being a pussy about this, not to mention selfish. At least you can find out what happened to your mom. She can't.

Slowly I resumed walking to the fridge, pulling it open and getting the cream out. Then I carried it over to the counter where I'd left the mugs of coffee and splashed some in. I stood there for a second looking down at the coffee mugs, my chest feeling tight. Wanting to put my fist through a wall or get on my bike or pull apart an engine or just carry Summer up to the bed and fuck her into the middle of next week.

Basically, do anything but think about those letters.

But they wouldn't let me alone and neither would her accusation. Yeah, fuck. She was right. I *was* being a pussy about this.

'Tiger, is that the reason you never learned to read? So you didn't have to find out what was in those letters?'

I blinked down at the mugs, the question bouncing around inside me like a pinball in a machine, hitting things, lighting things up.

Fuck, was she right?

'No,' I growled, denying the thought and trying to make it sound less like the lie it was. 'What the hell kind of pussy would that make me?'

'It wouldn't make you a pussy at all.' She sounded

very patient. 'That stuff is…hard. And you're trying to protect yourself.'

'I'm not a fucking kid,' I ground out, her tone irritating me. 'I'm not trying to protect myself. And I don't care why she left.'

'I think you do care,' she disagreed, unfazed by my shitty temper. 'Why else have you still got them? If you didn't care, you would have thrown that first letter away. But you didn't. You kept it. And then you kept all the rest, too.'

Jesus. Maybe she *was* right. Why *had* I kept them all this time? I didn't even know. I just knew that every time one came in the mail, I stuck it in the box with the others, closed it up and went on not thinking about them.

You kept them for a reason, douchebag.

Something curled up tight in my chest, a cold, uncomfortable feeling. It was familiar. The same one that had dogged me ever since I'd sat on my mother's bed in that empty apartment, listening for keys in the lock and the opening of the front door. Listening and hearing nothing but silence. Waiting all night for someone to come home, the cold feeling in my chest getting colder and colder, heavier and heavier as I realised that no one was coming home.

No one was ever coming home.

They'd left me and I didn't have the first fucking clue as to why.

So find out.

Ah, fuck.

'You told me that I wasn't to blame for my mom

leaving,' Summer said after a moment. 'Which means that you can't blame yourself for yours.'

I shut my eyes, tension crawling along my shoulders.

Maybe I really was afraid of what those letters would tell me and not being able to read was just a convenient excuse. Whatever, she was right about one thing: I needed to know once and for all what had happened to Mom and Tommy, not pretend the issue didn't exist the way I'd been doing for the last fifteen years of my life.

Summer had been able to face the stuff to do with her father, so what the hell was my excuse? I was a goddamn enforcer for the Knights of Ruin MC. I was a badass motherfucker. Yet I didn't want to read a bunch of letters from my own mother?

Fucking hell. What a dick I was.

You could find out where they are. You could see them.

Yeah, that was maybe a step too far. I was too angry, no point in denying it now. *Fucking* angry. I'd been telling myself for years that she must have had her reasons for leaving, for not telling me where she was going, and that I was okay with it.

But I wasn't okay with it. I never had been.

And one thing was for sure; I'd never be okay with it until I found out the truth of why she'd left and put the whole goddamn issue behind me once and for all.

I opened my eyes, picked up the mugs and strode over to where Summer sat, putting one down beside her. She watched me, her food untouched, blue eyes full of concern. Full of caring.

She shouldn't look at me like that. I wasn't her business.

'Eat,' I growled. 'And then you can read me those fucking letters.'

She blinked. 'Are you sure?'

'No. But you're right. I've got the chance to at least find out why she left so I should take it.'

Her expression softened, her mouth curving into the most beautiful fucking smile. Christ, she was like sunshine, sitting there in my shitty apartment, about to eat the meal I'd cooked for her. A ray of perfect sunshine, lighting the whole place up, making it brighter than it was before.

Making everything brighter than it was before.

That cold feeling in my chest began to fade away, melting like goddamn snow, leaving behind it heat.

I wanted to pull her across the counter, put my mouth on her, taste her sweetness. Have all that sunshine on me, covering me. Get it inside me somehow, so that cold feeling would never come back.

Dangerous, dumbass. She's not for you.

No, she wasn't.

But maybe for the next few hours she could be.

CHAPTER FIFTEEN

Summer

THE BREAKFAST TIGER cooked me was delicious and as we ate, he asked me about the job offer I had from the tech firm in Silicon Valley. I went on and on about it—probably way too long—but he seemed interested so I kept talking.

It was just so good to have someone interested in hearing what I had to say, someone who wasn't one of my professors, that I couldn't seem to shut myself up. And then he started asking about what I'd been studying at college and that was it, I started running at the mouth like a stuck faucet.

My head was telling me to shut the hell up, that he couldn't possibly be interested in all the math crap since it went over most people's heads, but he didn't tell me to shut the hell up. He didn't tell me it was boring and no one wanted to hear about it the way Dad did. No, it was the opposite. He seemed to get it, the fascination I had with numbers and the way they fit together.

I found myself describing equations and the excitement I got with solving them the way Dad talked about baseball, and Tiger's eyes didn't glaze over. And he didn't walk away. He asked questions, and even though I was pretty sure he didn't understand my answers, his mind seemed to work enough like mine that he grasped the basics of what I was saying.

More than that, he even seemed interested, offering his own perspective in the form of mechanics and the way he fixed engines. They were puzzles to him and I could see by the light in his eyes as he spoke that he loved solving those puzzles as much as I did.

It was so strange meeting someone who thought the way you did. Who was so different from you in every way on the surface, but underneath…

He was talking about how he'd got into fixing things, doing stuff with his hands since he was good at it and enjoyed doing something he was good at, and the spark in his eyes, in his whole face as he talked made my heart tighten.

Made it kick hard.

He was such an interesting man. Despite the biker macho stuff, he was articulate and thoughtful. And he listened to me, really listened.

This is all very bad news.

But I didn't want to think about that. I didn't want to think about what made my heart kick when I looked at him. I didn't want to think about what it might mean. In just a few days I would be flying to the West Coast and away from him, so there was no point letting myself hope for something that was never going to happen.

Better to enjoy this moment while I could.

We finished up breakfast and I helped him stack the plates in the dishwasher—or at least I tried. He chased me away and wouldn't let me, efficiently taking care of the dishes and mugs and wiping everything down.

I wanted to tease him about being a neat freak but suddenly remembered what I'd promised him after breakfast was over.

The letters he'd received from his mom. The ones he'd kept yet never read.

The ones that for some reason he was going to let me read to him.

I'd felt guilty about pushing him, especially when it was so obvious he didn't want to even think about those letters. But the stuff he'd said about me blaming myself for the way my own mother had left had stuck with me, making me wonder if he felt the same. But then, I *knew* he did. Why else would he be short-tempered about it every time I mentioned it? Why else would he be so angry?

And he *was* angry. I could see it in every line of his body.

This was a painful subject for him and me pushing him to deal with it probably hadn't helped.

As he finished up dealing with breakfast, he pointed at the couch. 'You go sit there. I'll go get the damn letters.'

So I went over to the couch and sat down while he went upstairs. He was up there awhile and I was starting to think that maybe I'd been wrong to push him. That my need to help him solve this puzzle had been a selfish one.

But then there was something inside me that knew he wasn't going to be able to get rid of the anger I'd seen in him, the pain, until he found out what was in those letters. I wanted him to get rid of the stuff that was hurting him. I wanted to help him be okay, the way he was helping me.

And maybe that *was* selfish, but if it helped him, then where was the harm?

He eventually came back down the stairs, holding a small cardboard box in his hands. His strongly carved features were a mask, but fire raged in his amber eyes.

He didn't give the box to me, merely set it on the coffee table in front of the couch, then he stood there with his arms folded across his broad inked chest. Radiating aggressiveness. He probably didn't realise that was what he was doing, but I could feel the tension and the anger pouring off him all the same.

As if this was a threat he was having to face down.

'Go on,' he said roughly. 'Take a look.'

I moved forward and grabbed the box, sitting back on the couch again. 'Do you want me to read it myself first, then read it out to you?'

'No.' The word was flat. 'I'm done running from this shit.'

He was scared, wasn't he? That was why he was so aggressive and so angry. He was scared about what was in those letters and what they would say.

It made my heart hurt for him. Made me angry at the woman who'd walked out and left her own son without even a word.

Well, there was no need to drag this out any longer than it needed to be.

Taking a breath, I opened the box and looked down. Neatly stacked inside were a bunch of yellowing envelopes. The one on the top was obviously the most recent one, judging by the date stamped on it, so I dug through the rest to get to the bottom of the pile and the first letter. Then I drew it out.

It had Tiger's name on it—Jake Clarke—and my hands shook a little as I opened the envelope and got out the letter inside.

I wanted to check there was nothing in there that might hurt him before I read it aloud, but he was standing there watching me, his golden eyes like a laser beam boring into me, and I knew I had to do what he said, to read out loud straight off.

"'Jake…'" I said, slowly reading out the tangled-up handwriting on the page. "'I know I took a long time to write this, and I know you probably won't be able to read it, but I have to tell you this. My conscience won't let me run away from it any more. I'm still a coward, though, writing a letter to you that I know you won't be able to read. But there's a reason for that.'"

I paused and swallowed, not daring to look at Tiger standing on the other side of the coffee table.

"'I had to leave, darling boy. And I couldn't tell you that I was going. It wasn't an easy decision to make, but I knew I had to do it. Protecting me, helping me, wasn't doing what was best for you. You deserved more than having to protect me all the time. You deserved more of a life than that. I should have told you I was going. I know I should have. But I was afraid you'd come after me. I was afraid you'd try to find me and I couldn't let you do that. So I took Tommy and I left. I wished he was old enough to stay with you, so he didn't have to be with me, but I couldn't let you have to be responsible for him, too. That wasn't the life I wanted for either of you. I'm sorry, Jake. I'm sorry I—'"

I broke off as, without a word, Tiger suddenly turned around, strode to the door of the warehouse, flung it open and walked through it.

My throat closed up tight, my eyes prickling with tears. I wanted to go to him to see if he was okay, but I wasn't sure I should. This wasn't my pain. It was his, and I didn't know whether that revelation had helped him or made it worse.

Was this the blame that he'd worried about? But it hadn't been anything he'd done. It was all his mother wanting to protect him. Sure, she'd used the most hurtful method possible, but it made sense in a twisted kind of way. I could see Tiger taking off after her, trying to find her. Not resting until he had.

But she'd wanted him to have a life. And this had clearly been the only way she could give it to him.

My heart clenched hard. I knew I shouldn't go after him, that this should be a private moment. But I wanted him to know that he wasn't alone. He'd been alone since his mother had left him—and, no, I didn't count his club because I couldn't see him sitting around with a bunch of bikers chatting about his pain—and I wanted him to know that I was here. That I knew a little of what it felt like. That I understood.

That he wasn't alone this time. He had me.

So I put the box back on the table and I stood up. And even though it was scary to intrude on something so deeply personal, I went after him. He'd chosen me to read those letters to him and that meant something, didn't it?

I walked over to the front door of the warehouse and peered outside. There was an enclosed concrete courtyard with other buildings on all sides and an entranceway just off the street. Tiger was standing in the middle of the courtyard with his back to me, his head bent, his arms at his sides and his hands in fists.

His body radiated tension and anger, and I couldn't stand leaving him there on his own. I closed the distance between us and I put a hand on his bare back, where some of those geometric tattoos overflowed from his shoulder and down to one shoulder blade.

His whole posture went even more tense, but he didn't move and he didn't say anything. And neither did I. I remained quiet and kept my hand on his back, letting him know I was here.

'I tried to think of what I'd done so many times.' His voice was so rough it hardly sounded like him. 'I went over and over that last day, that last week, thinking over what I'd done. Wondering. But there was nothing unusual. I remember just before I left the house that day, she kissed me on the forehead. She never did shit like that, because I didn't like it. But she did that day.'

I spread my hand out and pressed harder, giving him my presence and my warmth, his muscles still vibrating with tension.

'It was my fault in the end, though,' he went on.

'She *did* leave because of me. And she didn't even give me a choice about it.'

The note of pain in his voice got to me, burrowed inside me and stuck there like a thorn. I couldn't stop myself. I took my hand from his back and wound my arms around his waist, laying my cheek against his spine, inhaling his warmth and giving him back some of mine. 'No,' I said fiercely. 'It wasn't your fault. She left because she wanted what was best for you. I don't agree with her decision to leave without telling you, but it was her decision and there was nothing you could have done about it. She didn't leave because she didn't love you, Tiger. She left because she did.'

He didn't move, his strong back tense as a board. 'She wanted me to have a life.' There was bitterness tinging his words. 'But what did I do? I got into the MC. I fix motorcycles. That's it. What fucking life is that? I can't even goddamn read.'

I gripped him tighter. 'That's a hell of a life. You have a family of guys who look out for you and you do the work you love. Who else gets to do that? Who else gets to live the way they want? With no rules or restrictions? Isn't that what you love about the MC? You do what you like. You live free and fix bikes, solve puzzles. Sounds like a hell of a life to me.'

He said nothing for a long time, his muscles like steel beneath my cheek. Then his hands came down over mine where they were clasped on his taut stomach and he pushed them away. I let him, thinking he wanted distance.

But then he turned around sharply and before I

could move, his arms were around me and he was pulling me close, holding me against his hard, hot body. He turned his face into my hair and for a long moment he just stood there, keeping me tight in his arms.

I trembled, breathless. Hurting for him. Wanting to help him. So I raised my arms and put them around his neck and simply held him the way he was holding me.

For long moments we stood there, not saying a word, holding each other. And I closed my eyes, taking the moment to be with him. To inhale his scent and feel the strength of his arms around me, to feel the need in them, too. I didn't think he was a man who would ever accept comfort, but again he surprised me, squeezing me tight.

Then suddenly his head turned and his mouth was against my neck and he bit me. Not hard, but it sent an electric shock of sensation straight down my spine, making me gasp and shudder.

'I want you to fuck me,' he murmured against my skin. 'I want you to fuck me hard, and I want you to fuck me rough. Can you do that, baby girl?'

His words were a straight out aphrodisiac, firing directly between my thighs, making all the feelings that had gripped me as I'd given him that blow job come flooding back.

His hold on me shifted, his hands curving down under the hem of the T-shirt I wore, reminding me acutely that I had nothing on underneath it. His palms were hot against the bare skin of my butt as his finger curled around each cheek, squeezing me hard, pulling me against the front of his body, his hips flexing as he ground his pelvis against mine.

'Well?' he demanded, and there was a raw note that slid into me, gripping on as tightly as his hands on my ass.

'Yes,' I whispered, my voice as raw as his. 'Yes, I'll fuck you.'

He didn't say anything more. Instead he lifted me up as easily as he had the night before and carried me back into the warehouse. He didn't stop at the couch this time, carrying me straight up the stairs to the mezzanine floor where his big wide bed was.

Then set he set me down on it and stood back, undoing the zipper of his jeans with one hand as he stared down at me, his golden eyes burning. Heat and anger and pain and desire, all mixed together. He stood there almost arrogantly, unzipping his fly, his cock hard and ready as he pushed the denim down his narrow hips. My breath caught, watching the play of all that chiselled muscle and smooth skin. He wanted me to fuck him hard and rough...

I didn't know if I could do that. Could I?

Well, it didn't matter if I could or not. If that was what he wanted, what he needed, then that was what I'd give him. God knew, I didn't have much of anything else to give.

He stepped out of his jeans, naked and strong and so beautiful I could hardly breathe. Then he moved over to where I sat and he pulled the T-shirt off me so I was naked, too. He pushed me back on the bed and came down onto it with me, crouching above me on all fours, just like the tiger that prowled up his arm. Hungry and feral and predatory.

I put my hands up, pressing my palms to his hard, hot chest. 'I thought I was going to be the one to fuck you hard,' I said unsteadily.

His mouth curved in a smile that had nothing to do with amusement, all challenge and fire and not a bit of desperation. 'So do it, baby girl.'

That desperation switched something on inside me, something aggressive I hadn't known was there. He wanted me. He wanted *me*. I'd been worried about whether I could handle him and I had. I damn well had.

Now I wanted to make him wonder whether or not he could handle *me*.

So I shoved at him—hard. 'On your back, big boy.'

His smile deepened and this time there was definitely a hint of amusement in it. 'Big boy?'

I ignored him, shoving at him again. 'If you don't get on your back, you don't get any p-pussy.' Which would have sounded hotter if I hadn't stuttered over the word, or blushed like a teenager, but, hell, I'd said it. My first dirty talk. Yay me.

Still grinning, he pushed himself away from me and turned over on his back, putting his hands behind his head like he was lying on a beach. 'Here I am. Doing what you say. Where's my pussy then?'

I sat up and before I could second-guess myself, I straddled him, easing my sex up against the hard ridge of his cock. It was long and thick and as hot as he was and it made me shiver. 'Here's your pussy.'

I put my hands on the pillows on either side of his head, looking down into his fascinating eyes, the tips of my nipples brushing against his chest. Then I shifted my hips. 'Can you feel it?'

Golden flames leapt in his gaze and I heard the breath go out of him, and that was as massive a turn-on as the pressure of his cock against my sex.

'Oh, yeah,' he breathed, all thick and intense. 'I feel it. Give me more.'

There was something amazingly powerful about having this tall strong, muscled and dangerous biker underneath me. Looking at me like there was nothing and no one else in the entire world. Looking at me like he'd die if he didn't have me right there and then.

It made me want to play with him. He might want it hard and rough, but he was going to have to wait first.

I flexed my hips again, rubbing myself against him, feeling the line of pleasure pull taut inside me, a dragging sensation that made me want to pant.

'Yeah,' he whispered, staring up at me like I was the sun and he'd spent a lifetime in the dark. 'Just like that. More, baby girl.'

I held his gaze, lowering my head so my hair curtained us, falling over his shoulders. He tried to lift up to kiss me, but I pulled back, tantalising him. His beautiful mouth curved again, like he knew exactly what I was doing and approved. So I shifted my hips once more, giving him back a taste of what he'd given me the night before in his room. The night that felt like so long ago but really wasn't.

He made a deep noise in his throat as I ground

myself against him, moving along that delicious hard ridge, rubbing my clit against it, panting and gasping in response. 'You like that?' I heard myself say. 'You like this pussy against your hard cock?'

'What do you think?' He lifted his head impatiently, trying to kiss me, but I pulled away again, brushing my nipples against his chest, tantalising him even more.

'Not yet.' I let my mouth hover bare inches above his. 'Beg me for a kiss and I might give you one.'

But of course he cheated. He lifted his head and took that kiss anyway, his mouth hard and demanding. His hands were on my hips, pressing me more insistently against him, his pelvis lifting against mine. And for a second I fell into the kiss, into the heat of him, letting him do whatever he wanted.

'Condom,' he murmured against my mouth. 'Now.'

I knew where they were, having watched him put more than a couple on himself the night before. So I reached over the side of the bed to the small nightstand and pulled open the drawer. He stroked me as I did, one hand curving around my butt, the other finding my breast and flicking my nipple with his thumb.

I shuddered as I pulled the packet out, his touch making the breath catch in my throat and sensation spread like wildfire over my skin. I sat back, ripping open the foil and taking out the condom.

He watched me from beneath black lashes, his gaze hotter than that wildfire sweeping over me. It filled me with power, made me feel like I could do anything, so I didn't freak out that I hadn't put a condom on a guy before. I didn't doubt myself. It was a puzzle to be solved and I solved it simply by putting it on him and rolling the latex down with my hands.

He made another of those deep, delicious sounds in his throat, lifting his hips up into my hands, making it obvious how much he liked my touch. It was such a thrill I wanted to do it again and again, wring some more of those sounds from him.

But there was something I wanted more.

Him. Inside me. Hard and deep and rough like he wanted.

I grabbed his cock, meeting his gaze, holding it. 'You want this pussy?' I teased him, rubbing the head of his dick against the throbbing flesh between my thighs, making him sweat.

'Fuck, yes.' His voice was rough, guttural. 'Do it. Give it to me.'

I gave him a slow, sensual smile and squeezed him. 'Say please.'

His breath hissed. 'You fucking tease. I love it.' He lifted his hips, trying to arch up into me, and I squeezed him again, making him groan. 'Please, baby girl. Please fuck me. *Now*.'

God, he was *so* hot. His desperation was such a turn-on that abruptly I lost interest in teasing him, wanting him inside me.

So I lifted myself up and guided him inside, both of us shuddering as I slid down on him, feeling the delicious stretch of him inside me, the burn as he filled me. He was big and I loved it, the intensity of the sensation making me gasp as he impaled me completely.

I put my hands on his chest, balancing myself,

his fingers on my hips, digging in. I looked into his eyes, saw the heat, the need there, and knew he saw the same in mine. The connection was intense and made me tremble, but I didn't look away. He wanted this hard and rough, and he was going to get it.

His hands tightened, but I shook my head. 'No. Let me figure it out.'

'Don't know if I can wait that long.' His lips peeled back in a feral grimace. 'I need you fucking me right now.'

Digging my nails into his chest, I moved experimentally, watching the expression of agonised pleasure cross his face as I did so.

'Oh, yeah, Jesus. Keep doing that.'

I kind of wanted not to, to do something different to shock him, but it felt too good and I was rapidly getting to the point where I wanted the pleasure of him as much as he wanted the pleasure of me.

So I did what he liked, again and again, finding a rhythm that made us both groan. A slow rise and fall, the feeling of his cock sliding in and out making me shiver and shake. I spread my hands out on his chest, moving faster, harder, and he gave me a savage grin. 'Fuck, yes. Ride me, baby girl. Show me what you got.'

So I showed him. Riding him even faster, lifting myself up and slamming myself down on him, digging my nails into his chest so I left little circles on his flesh. Marking him. And he did the same to me with his hands on my hips, holding me so tightly he was going to leave bruises.

I wanted those bruises. I wanted those marks. I

wanted to be branded by this time with him. So I'd carry it with me when I flew away from him and into the new life I was going to have.

So I'd never forget.

Not that I needed those marks.

I'd never forget Tiger. Never. Not as long as I lived.

My heart was thundering in my head and I was moving rhythmically. The slick glide of him inside me driving us both out of our minds. In. Out. Up. Down.

Harder. Faster. The sounds of his flesh slamming into mine and the gasping of our breath echoing around us.

So good. So good.

I fucked him as hard and as rough as I could, and I looked into his eyes the whole time. And I saw the moment he came, golden fire exploding, the roar of my name shuddering against the ceiling.

Then he put his hand between my thighs and pressed down hard on my clit, bringing me into the flames with him.

CHAPTER SIXTEEN

Tiger

I LAY ON the bed, panting and fucking destroyed. Because that was what she'd done to me. She'd destroyed me. She'd done exactly what I told her to, fucked me hard and rough, and now I wasn't sure I'd ever be the same again.

She'd collapsed on top of me, her soft hair all over my chest, and I could still feel her hot little pussy squeezing my cock. Christ, she was amazing. Everything about her was amazing. I wanted to hold her tightly to me, never let her go. She was mine, which was a fucking weird thought since I'd never had it before about anyone.

She knew about my past, about my mother. And she'd been the one to read that letter to me, discovering right along with me the real reason Mom had left.

That had been the hardest thing to hear. To know that Mom had gone to protect me. To give me a fucking life, as if I didn't have one already. I'd been full of nothing but anger in that moment, because it *had* been my fault she'd gone. And if she'd given me the choice, I would have told her not to go, that the decisions about my life were mine to make, not hers. But, no, she'd taken the choice from me. She'd decided to leave me without even talking to me first and I'd wanted to smack something so bad I hadn't been able to think straight.

I'd had to walk out, to leave before I did something stupid and frightened Summer.

I hadn't expected Summer to come after me. To follow and put a hand on my back. Her warmth had been astonishing and her voice calm.

Then she'd put her arms around me, her warmth soaking into me, and it was the strangest fucking thing. No one had ever given me a hug before, not since Mom left, and it made me feel… Christ, I don't even know. Like I wanted to melt back into her. She'd felt strong at my back and it was as if she was giving me a piece of her own strength, filling up something that had always felt hollow and empty before.

Jesus, how had she ever thought of herself as weak? I was the one who was weak and now she was making me strong.

I hadn't wanted to talk about it any more right then. I'd just wanted her.

Fucking hell, I'd never wanted anything so badly in my life.

Then she'd given me more than strength. She'd given me the fire that I knew was inside her, that burning blue spark. Riding me like I was her favourite stallion. So fucking hot.

I hadn't realised what I was missing—that I'd been missing anything at all, in fact—until she'd put her hands on my chest and looked down into my eyes. Holding my gaze as she'd fucking taken me to heaven and back.

Hot and fierce and bright. That was Summer. And I wanted more.

I tightened my arms around her.

She's yours now.

Yeah, she was. She just fucking was. And suddenly it didn't feel weird. It felt right, like it was meant to be somehow.

Keep would probably be after me by now and I thought I'd better check in with him. No, it was going to be more than a check in. It was going to be a fucking full-on denial. There was no way I'd let Summer anywhere near her father. Anywhere near *anyone* who could hurt her.

I was going to protect her until it was time for her to fly out west to her new job and her new life, and if anyone tried to stop her they'd have to answer to me.

I rolled onto my side, taking her with me. Then I pushed her onto her back, sifting her beautiful hair through my fingers. Felt like fucking silk. 'I need to go check in with Keep,' I murmured. 'Don't worry, I won't mention you're here. I'll hide you until it's time to get your flight and then I'll take you to the airport myself.'

Her brow creased, an expression I couldn't quite catch flashing over her face. 'Are you sure? You'd really lie to your president for me?'

'Nothing I haven't done already, baby girl.'

'But your club—'

I put a finger over her mouth, silencing her. 'Leave the club to me. It's my thing, I'll handle it, okay?'

'Okay.' Yet that worried look didn't leave her eyes. 'Tiger, I'm sorry. I don't want to make things difficult for you.'

'Yeah, I know. But that's not your decision to make. It's mine. And I'm making it right now.'

Another flicker of expression across her lovely face. 'Okay,' she said again, sounding reluctant. 'But you know, if there's anything—'

I shut her up by kissing her, sliding my tongue into her mouth so she couldn't speak. And then she didn't want to anyway, giving a little groan and tipping her head back, encouraging me to kiss her deeper, harder.

I growled, because I wanted to. But I had to deal with Keep first.

Giving her a nip, I lifted my head and gently disengaged myself from her, rolling away to deal with the condom in the nearby wastebasket. 'I need to call Keep.' I turned and gave her a look from over my shoulder. 'Don't go anywhere, okay? And definitely don't get dressed. I have plans for you.'

She flushed, which was straight out weird considering what she'd done to me not two minutes ago, but I was fucking delighted all the same. I was already getting hard thinking of all the other dirty ways I was going to make her come today.

Christ, suddenly two days with her didn't seem enough.

I pulled on my jeans and grabbed my phone, taking it downstairs so I wouldn't stress her out. Then I hit Keep's number.

He answered it almost immediately. 'Where the fuck have you been and why aren't you answering my goddamn calls?'

'I've been out looking for the chief's daughter, just like you wanted, Prez,' I lied without even a twinge of guilt. 'And, no, I haven't found her yet. Anyone else?'

'No,' Keep said curtly. 'Chief's getting fucking pissed, put out a few APBs, all kinds of shit. You don't have a number for her or anything?'

'Why? Because I did some protection for her? That was five years ago. Fuck only knows what's up with her now.'

Keep grunted. 'Yeah, okay. Well, keep your eyes open.'

He ended the call without another word, but I didn't lose any sleep over it. I had no problem with protecting Summer. None at all. And it was kind of weird to think that I didn't. Because it meant that she had become more important to me than the club, which was a worry, but I decided I wasn't going to let that get to me. I could deal with that later, once she'd got safely away. Right now, I had other things to do.

Like making her come some more.

We spent the rest of the day in bed, pausing only for a lunch break and then some sleep in the afternoon. I woke her up after that, flipping her over onto her stomach and pulling her up on her hands and knees. Then I ate her out from behind, making her come a couple of times, before pulling those slender hips up against mine and sliding deep inside her quivering little pussy.

It was hard and it was raw and I made her scream. Then I made her scream some more before I let myself go, pushing her down and slamming her into the mattress over and over until I was blind with the fucking ecstasy of it.

I got her up after that and took her into the shower again, soaping her down, loving the feel of her leaning against me as if she couldn't stand upright on her own, knowing it was me who'd made her feel that.

Afterwards I made her dinner and we sat at the counter and talked about nothing in particular. I liked hearing her talk about her new job and about her interest in math. It all went over my head—she was so fucking smart it kind of astounded me—but she explained everything in such an easy way it was almost as if I could grasp it. She talked about her life at college and then, when she got sick of talking about herself, she began to ask me about life at the club and what it was like.

I was honest with her, didn't gloss over the stuff that wasn't great, but she seemed to get how important the club was to me. How like a family it was. How my brothers truly were like brothers.

After I'd given her a rundown on one of our wilder parties, making her blue eyes go round and her cheeks pink, I took her over to the workshop and showed her a few of the bikes I was in the process of fixing. She was right into it, peering at everything and asking me questions, wanting to know how things worked.

I'd never explained any mechanical shit to a woman before, let alone one who was so interested. She even sat down beside me, watching and getting me to explain what I was doing, making comments and asking yet more questions.

I didn't much like it when people talked at me while I was working, but with Summer I found I didn't care. In fact, I liked it. I liked that she was interested in something that interested me, too, and that it was all completely genuine. There wasn't a fake bone in her body, not one.

A couple of hours passed like that and it was… good. Just fucking good.

Later, I got us both beers and sat on the couch with her in my lap, talking about nothing. Talking about everything.

I was so deep in discussion with her about something she called game theory that I didn't even hear the distinctive rumble of a hog in the courtyard outside. All I knew was that one minute we were alone and talking, the next the door of my warehouse had been kicked open and Keep was there, striding inside with Smoke following along behind him.

For a second Summer and I just stared at them in shock, because what the actual fuck? Then she stiffened in my lap, making a soft, distressed sound.

And I acted without thought.

Pushing her off my lap, I shoved her behind me, then stood up, putting myself between my president and my best buddy, and her.

Keep stopped not far from me, his blue eyes glittering and full of rage. 'What the fuck do you think you're doing?' he demanded, coming straight out with it.

I met him stare for fucking stare. 'I could ask you the same thing.'

Stupid question. There was only one reason he was here and she was sitting on the couch behind me, dressed only in my T-shirt.

A sudden rush of possessiveness filled me. I didn't want these assholes looking at her. I didn't want them even glancing in her direction, so I adjusted my stance, blocking her from them as much as I could. 'What the fuck, Prez?' I decided to go on the attack, since there was no point denying Summer's presence here. 'I'm just having a quiet beer with—'

'The chief of police's daughter,' Keep finished, hard and cold. 'The one you told me you were out looking for.'

Summer started to say something, but I held up my hand sharply to let her know that her talking right now was a very bad idea.

Luckily she seemed to get it and stayed quiet.

'I didn't tell him,' Smoke said from his position behind Keep, his dark gaze meeting mine. 'Crash let it slip this afternoon that she'd been at the party yesterday. We came to ask you where she was.'

Rage turned over inside me. Crash. Of course. That fucking asshole. I thought he hadn't known who she was but clearly he had. 'Why?' I demanded. 'He want some brownie points from you, Prez?'

'Doesn't matter why.' There was nothing but ice in Keep's voice. Always a very bad fucking sign. 'You knew who she was. You knew she was nothing but trouble for the fucking club, and not only did you *not* tell me you had her, you've been fucking her, too, from the looks of things.' The glitter in his eyes got even colder. 'You lied to me, Tiger.'

Aggression poured through my veins. Because he was right, I'd done those things. I'd lied to my president. I'd broken his trust. I'd created a potentially volatile situation for my club, one we really didn't need right now.

I'd fucked up.

And I didn't even care.

There was only one thing I did care about right in that moment and she was sitting right behind me.

The truth of it hit me so fucking hard that I couldn't speak but I knew.

It was her. It was Summer. She was mine.

And I wasn't giving her up, not to anyone.

'Yeah, I did.' I didn't bother keeping the edge out of my voice. 'I did lie to you. But I did it to protect her.'

Keep's expression hardened. 'I don't give a fuck why you did it. That doesn't change the fact that you did.' The look on his face got even meaner. 'I got no room in my club for an officer who lies to his president. I got no patience with that shit.'

'Prez—' Smoke began.

But Keep gave a jerk of his head, silencing him. 'You want to make things right, Tiger?' His blue gaze was squarely on mine. 'You take her to Grant right the fuck now.'

I didn't make the mistake of thinking this wasn't the flat-out choice that it was. Basically, it was her or the club. The club that'd looked out for me, been there for me, that'd been my family since my mom left. Or a woman I'd only really known a matter of days, yet who'd somehow lit up my life in a way no one else ever had.

I didn't even have to think. I already knew my choice.

'No,' I said flatly 'She stays with me.'

Keep smiled and it wasn't a nice smile. It was his 'don't fuck with the president' smile. 'You're seriously going to choose her? Over your club?'

Smoke was silent, giving me a strange look that seemed a whole lot like understanding.

But I couldn't deal with that now. There was only Keep and the knowledge that if he took one step towards the woman behind me, I was going to punch his fucking head in. Which would be crossing a line.

I couldn't come back from that and I knew it. But again, I didn't give a shit. Protecting her was more important. *She* was more important.

More important than the club. More important than me.

More important than any damn thing.

So I put my shoulders back and my hands curled into fists, and I stared at Keep, daring him to come at me. To touch what was fucking mine.

And the tension in the warehouse wound so tight with violence it was a wonder the whole fucking thing didn't explode.

Then there came a sound from behind me, and suddenly Summer was coming around me, putting herself between me and Keep.

'Summer,' I began, reaching out for her. 'What the fuck are you—'

'I'll go with you,' she said flatly, not even looking at me, all her attention on Keep. 'If you want me to go, I'll go right now.'

CHAPTER SEVENTEEN

Summer

I STOOD THERE looking into the cold blue eyes of the Knights of Ruin's president and I'd never felt so terrified in all my stupid life. But I'd known from the moment he'd stormed into Tiger's warehouse that this was what I had to do.

I couldn't let Tiger take the fall for me. I couldn't let him choose between the club that was his entire family and me, a woman he hadn't known for very long. After all, this had all been my fault. I was the one who'd run to the clubhouse. I was the one who'd asked him to keep me hidden. Sure, it had been his choice to hide me, but I was the one who'd put him in this position in the first place.

So no. He wasn't going to have to choose.

It was time for me to face the consequences of what I'd done.

It was time for me to face my father.

'Don't you dare,' Tiger said from behind me. 'Don't you fucking dare, Summer.'

I could feel his heat and then suddenly he was

gripping my upper arms and turning me to face him. His gaze was full of angry flames, his expression burning with intensity. 'Don't say a fucking word,' he growled. 'In fact, get your ass up the stairs and don't come down until I say.'

I knew he was trying to protect me. I could see it in his eyes. And there was a very large part of me that wanted to do exactly what he said.

But I wasn't going to.

If I didn't do this right now, if I didn't face my fear of my father, it would dog me for the rest of my life. And who knew who else it would involve? Who knew who else would get hurt? It had hurt Tiger already, I knew it had, and I couldn't stand it. I *wouldn't* stand it.

So I simply stared back at him, letting him see that I wasn't going to back down on this. 'Let me go, Tiger.'

'No.' His fingers tightened, the look in his eyes blazing. 'You're fucking mine now. You're not going anywhere.'

My heart threw itself against my ribs, because there was nothing more I wanted in that moment than to be his. No one had ever wanted me the way he did. No one had ever said it out loud, with other people watching, claiming me for themselves.

I wanted to say 'Okay, I'm yours' so badly I could taste it.

But I couldn't. I didn't want him to have to choose. I didn't want him to have to deal with the consequences of my own cowardice.

He deserved better than that.

He deserves better than you.

The thought whispered through my head and I knew it was true. Because even if all this stuff with Keep hadn't happened, nothing changed the fact that I would be leaving him soon anyway, flying thousands of miles away from him permanently.

I couldn't stay. I wasn't part of his world and I never would be, and I was tired of being where I didn't fit. Where I was invisible.

I wanted to take the job, create a life of my own, and even though the thought of him coming with me made me light-headed with happiness, I knew I couldn't ask him to. Again, I didn't want him to have to choose between me and the life and the family he'd built here for himself. And I didn't want to have to leave him like his mother had left him.

'I'm not.' I struggled to keep my voice level. 'I have to go, Tiger. I *have* to.'

'No, you don't.' His fingers tightened even more, pulling me up against him, his grip almost painful. 'Stay here. I'll protect you.'

'I don't want you to protect me.' My throat felt tight and dry, my body beginning to blaze in response to the heat of his so close. 'I have to face Dad. I can't run away from him any more.'

'I'll come with you. I'll make sure—'

'No,' I cut him off sharply, meeting his gold gaze. 'I have to do it on my own. This is my issue to deal with, not yours.'

He growled, full on, like the big cat prowling up his arm, jerking me even closer to him. Then he bared his teeth, trying to intimidate me. 'Fuck you.

Your issues are mine now and I'll help you deal with them whether you like it or not.'

'If I don't do this now, on my own, I'll always be scared.' I kept my gaze on his, willing him to understand. 'I'll always be hiding. I have to face him and I have to do it without you.'

He was silent a long moment, staring at me. 'But you'll come back. And we'll have the last few days together, right?'

My throat closed up and there was a weight on my chest, so heavy.

The last few days. All two of them.

It's not enough.

No, it wasn't. There would never be enough time in the whole world to be with Tiger. I didn't want two days. I wanted forever. But would he? Sure, he wanted to protect me, and he wanted another couple of days of hot sex, but in the end, would he see me off at the airport without a backward glance?

My heart twisted inside my chest at the thought, painful and tight. And in that moment I knew I couldn't do it. I couldn't come back to him. Because if I did, I'd never want to leave. I'd want to stay here with him forever. Except he didn't strike me as a forever kind of guy. Sure, we'd had hot sex and some great conversations, but I was positive he didn't feel the same way about me as I did about him. And, really, why should he?

I was a nerdy girl who liked math and who wasn't anything special. Not to a guy like him.

Perhaps it would be better to save us both the trouble and not come back at all.

Coward.

Yeah, well, that's what I was, wasn't I?

I'd deal with my father. I could handle that. But maybe I couldn't handle Tiger after all.

'No,' I said shakily, forcing the word out. 'I don't think that's a good idea.'

Something leapt in his gaze, a blaze of anger. 'What do you mean you don't think that's a good idea? It's what I want. I thought that's what you wanted, too?'

I was beginning to tremble now. 'Well… I—I've changed my mind.' It was harder than I thought to say it. Harder still with his fierce amber eyes on mine. 'I think it's b-better if we call it quits now.'

For a second something blinding flicked in his gaze, a bright flash of something I didn't recognise. It made my chest hurt, made my pulse start to climb, made me want to tell him I was lying, that I never wanted to call it quits. But I couldn't.

It was easier this way.

Easier for you, coward.

'You really want that?' He searched my face as if looking for something. 'You don't even want another day?' A raw note had crept into his voice and it felt like a knife in my heart.

But I'd made my decision. It was better to be the one who walked away than the one left behind, as I knew all too well.

So does he.

He did. But he was stronger than I was. He always had been.

'No.' It came out as a whisper and I don't even know how I managed to say it. 'I don't.'

Tiger shut down then. I could see the moment it happened. Like a door slamming in my face, shutting out all the heat from his amber eyes, leaving me alone in the cold, with nothing but ashes.

He released me, so quickly I nearly stumbled back. 'If that's what you want.' His voice was absolutely expressionless, his face hard and set. 'You'd better go then. Say hi to your daddy for me.' He flicked a glance at Keep and his friend Smoke. 'You pricks can fuck off, too.'

I hated the expression on his face, and it was agony to know that I'd put it there. 'I...just think this is the easiest way,' I began hoarsely, wanting to explain so he understood.

But he didn't let me. 'I don't want to hear it.' The amber of his gaze had dulled. 'Just go.'

'Tiger—'

'Yours isn't the only pussy in the world, Summer. It certainly isn't going to be the last.'

I hated the flat sound in his voice and I reached out to him, but he'd already turned to his workshop area. 'Have a nice trip. Enjoy your new job.'

The knife in my heart turned, a vicious pain.

'Enough of this bullshit.' Keep's deep voice from behind me. 'You coming with us, Summer?'

Tiger had gone to one of the bikes, the one I'd watched him work on only a couple of hours ago, his clever hands moving with a kind of knowledge and skill that had thrilled me.

There were tears in my eyes, my stupid heart

wanting him to come after me, to fight for me, to insist I was his and that he wasn't going to let me go.

But he didn't.

'Yes,' I croaked. 'I'll just get dressed.'

I got my clothes together, then I went into the bathroom for some privacy to get changed, trying to blink back the tears that kept wanting to fall. It was awful, the thought of taking his shirt off, of not being close to his familiar scent and warmth, so because I was selfish at heart, I kept it on, pulling on my underwear and denim mini to go with it.

Then I came back outside to find Keep waiting at the front door of the warehouse. Smoke was down the other end with Tiger, who was bent over one of the bikes. He didn't look up. Not once.

I felt cold and the pain in my chest wouldn't stop throbbing, but I tried to ignore it.

This was the right decision. It was.

Keep eyed me as I approached and perhaps I should have been afraid of him, but I couldn't bring myself to care. Instead I simply met his cold blue gaze and said, 'You tell my dad Tiger found me. And he called you the moment he did.'

Keep raised one brow. 'Why the fuck would I do that?'

I didn't even flinch. 'Because I said.'

He gave me another long look and I knew I was treading on thin ice. But all he said was 'Okay.' And the next minute he was leading me outside to where his bike was parked.

I got on it and as we roared out of the courtyard, I didn't look back.

It felt like I'd left a piece of myself with Tiger and I didn't look to know which piece it was.

Stupid thing was I already knew.

My idiot heart.

Keep took me home, right to my front door. He didn't say a word to me the whole time, waiting silently beside me until the door opened and there was Dad standing on the threshold.

'Tiger found your girl,' Keep said shortly to him. 'You might want to take better care of her in future.'

Dad opened his mouth to say something, but Keep had already turned around and was off down the steps, leaving me there with my father.

He'd always seemed tall to me, and intimidating, his blue eyes full of a fury that never seemed to go away. He turned that fury on me now. 'Where *the hell* have you been?' he demanded angrily. 'Get in the goddamn house.'

Normally when he got angry like this, all I wanted to do was run away and hide, make myself invisible so he wouldn't see me.

But now...now I could feel my own rage start to rise, thick and hot, fuelled by the pain in my heart at leaving Tiger and by the unfairness of it all. How dare he tell me what to do? How *dare* he threaten Tiger and Tiger's club way he had? What gave him the right? Just because I was his daughter, it didn't mean he could treat me like a possession or use me as a weapon against the people I cared about.

The only power he has over you is the power you give him, so don't give it to him...

Tiger's words echoed in my head and, despite the heartbreak I'd just left behind, I straightened my spine, firmed my shoulders.

No, I wasn't going to run away and hide. I wasn't going to be goddamn invisible, not this time, not today.

Today I was going to deal with him once and for all.

'No,' I said flatly. 'I will not get in the goddamn house.'

Dad's head snapped back. 'What did you say?'

'You heard me.' I met his furious blue gaze, held it. 'My days of doing whatever you say are over.'

He had one hand on the doorframe and his knuckles turned white as an expression of pure fury crossed his face. 'You ungrateful little bitch. You run away for days on end and now you think you can—'

'I think I can do whatever the hell I want!' My own fury leapt high and I let it, taking a step forward, getting right in his face. 'In fact, now it's *my* turn to tell *you* what to do. First of all, you're going to leave Tiger alone completely, and if I *ever* hear of you threatening either him or his club, you will never see me again.'

My father took a half step back, then stopped, as if realising what he was doing. He scowled, puffing his chest up. 'Are you threatening me?'

I ignored him. 'Second, I'm taking that job whether you like it or not. And if you try to stop me, I'll lay charges. Because I know there's at least a couple of good guys at the station who aren't in your pocket.'

'You really think you can—'

'Third.' I took another step, getting closer, holding his gaze, letting him see my strength, my rage, the broken heart in my chest fuel to the fire. 'Don't you ever try to manipulate me again. You've been doing that all my life and it ends right here, right now.'

For the first time, uncertainty flickered behind the anger in his eyes, and to my surprise it was he who took another step back, as if I was the one intimidating him. 'Jesus Christ, girl,' he blustered. 'What gives you the right to talk to me like that? I gave you a roof over your head. I gave you food on your plate and the clothes on your back. After your mother left—'

'You blamed me for her leaving,' I finished for him, anger becoming a strength flowing through me, the strength Tiger had always told me I possessed and yet I'd never felt. Not until this moment. 'You made sure to tell me she left because of me every single goddamn day.'

He said nothing, his mouth gone flat and hard in that tight line, every inch of him the disapproving police chief.

'Fourth, you want to know why I'm really here, Dad?' I lifted my chin. 'I'm here to tell you that you're wrong. Mom didn't leave because of me. She left because you're a bully. A controlling, manipulative prick. It was *your* fault she went away, not mine, and I'm not taking the blame for you any more.'

More fury leapt in his gaze, but he kept the distance between us. And I realised with a shock that it was because he was afraid.

He was afraid of *me*.

'You know why she never came back?' he said suddenly, the look on his face turning vicious. 'Because I told her if she did, I'd take you away where she could never find us.'

It felt like he'd kicked me in the stomach.

I stood there for a moment, the breath knocked out of me, staring at his familiar face, at the lines of bitterness around his eyes and mouth, the deep folds of anger and resentment along the once-sharp jawline.

Pain coiled inside me. 'Why? Why the hell would you do that?'

'Why do you think?' That viciousness lingered in his voice. 'Because the bitch left me and she needed to be punished.'

He'd been handsome once, my dad. A proud, intimidating figure. But he wasn't now. Suddenly all I saw in front of me was an old man, twisted and bitter and mean. A man with no power who was trying to get some however he could.

A weak, hollow kind of man.

This was who'd I'd been afraid of for so long? *This?*

Tiger had told me all this time not to give him any power but this was the first time I'd truly felt it in my heart. Truly seen that far from being this powerful, scary figure, my father had had no power to start with.

Dear God. How could I have let this small, weak man dictate my life?

Especially when I knew—I just *knew*—how much stronger than him I was.

All the air rushed suddenly back into my lungs,

the realisation making me feel like I'd been suffocating all these years and only now could I breathe.

Dad's confession would have broken the Summer that I'd been a week ago. But I wasn't that woman any more. I'd spent three days in the arms of one of the toughest, most frightening men I knew and he'd made me feel like a goddess. He'd made me feel wanted in a way I'd never felt before. He made me feel truly strong.

Because he made me feel loved.

It hit me then, like a bolt of white lightning, how unimportant standing on this step was. How unimportant my father was. That the only person who mattered to me was the man I'd left behind.

And I'd left him because I'd still been scared little Summer Grant, who'd had so little faith in herself and her own feelings that she'd rather walk away than fight for what she wanted.

Dad was blustering, making all kinds of threats, but they slipped off me like rain off an umbrella. They didn't even touch me.

I simply turned around and walked away.

Because there was only one thing I wanted and he'd been left behind by everyone who'd loved him.

I was *not* going to be another.

CHAPTER EIGHTEEN

Tiger

'YOU'RE A DUMBASS,' Smoke said.

I ignored him and kept myself bent over the bike, concentrating hard on the engine and not on whatever it was that kept kicking me hard in the chest, over and over again.

I didn't want to fix the fucking bike. I wanted to smash it. I wanted to knock the whole fucking thing off its stand and watch it crash down. Then maybe smash the headlight and kick the chrome of the exhaust. Take a sledgehammer to the petrol tank, just fucking destroy that motherfucker.

I didn't even know why.

Sure you do, asshole.

Yeah, okay, so I did. I wanted to destroy that bike the way Summer had fucking destroyed me.

Christ, I don't know what I'd expected. Not for her to give herself up like that, that was for sure. Not for her to give me some bullshit about not wanting me to choose between her and the club. And then to say she didn't want to come back to me, not have those couple of extra days before she left...

Fucked if I knew what that was all about. I'd thought she'd wanted it just like I did, but to have her change her mind like that didn't make any sense.

You should have asked her.

Yeah, maybe I should have. But, fuck, if she didn't want me, she didn't want me. I wasn't going to insist. Plenty more pussy in the sea and all that shit.

'I said you're a dumbass.'

I bared my teeth at the engine. 'Fuck off.'

Annoyingly, Smoke stayed right where he was. Prick didn't know when to take a hint. 'Why did you let her go?'

'Didn't you hear me?' I picked up a wrench and tried twisting off a nut. 'I said fuck off.'

'You wanted her, right?'

The wrench slipped and I dropped it. 'Fuck.' I kicked the fucking thing across the ground. 'Motherfucking fuck!'

Smoke stuck his hands into his pockets. 'Are you finished being a damn drama queen?'

I raised a fist, ready to do some damage to something or, preferably, someone. 'Don't make me fucking hit you.'

He didn't even look at my fist. 'Like I said, why did you let her go?'

I could feel my heartbeat raging, the effort it took to keep myself under control slipping, my raised fist shaking. And I didn't want to admit to why. 'Because she wanted to fucking go, okay?'

He gave me another of those long, steady looks. 'You said she was yours.'

'I was wrong.'

'No, you weren't.' He didn't move, didn't even blink. 'You're in love with her.'

The words hit me like a tank rolling the fuck over me, crushing me into the dirt.

He's right. That's why you want to destroy things. Because she left you.

I wanted to deny it, wanted to roar that it was a fucking lie, that I didn't love her. That she was just another girl I'd fucked and had a good time with but didn't give a shit about.

But that lie wouldn't come.

Of course he was right. Of course I was in love with her. And it was tearing me apart.

'What the fuck has that got to do with anything?' I demanded.

'You let her go.'

'What the fuck was I supposed to do? Chain her to my bed?'

Smoke said nothing for a moment and I found myself fighting to breathe. Because my chest hurt. Everything fucking hurt.

'Go after her then,' he said, as if it was easy. 'You want her, go get her.'

'No. She made her choice and it wasn't me. So I'm making my choice now. And that's to let her the fuck go.'

His mouth twisted. 'You know what you sound like? You sound like me when I had to leave Cat. I was trying to protect her, making all these dumb fucking excuses about why I couldn't have her. Telling myself it was to keep her and Annie safe. But it wasn't. I was just afraid. Afraid of what I wanted and what it would mean.'

'It's not fucking the same,' I snarled.

'Yeah, dumb fuck, it is. You're making a whole lot of excuses about why you let her go. Why you can't go after her now. But don't kid yourself they're actually the reasons you're doing this. The real reason you're not is because you're in love and you don't know what to do about it, and you're shitting yourself.'

I didn't want to hear that. I didn't want to hear anything of what he said. 'Just because you've got yourself an old lady it doesn't make you some fucking love guru.' I kicked at the bike stand, the machine wobbling. 'Now, why don't you fuck off before I call the police about some asshole trespassing on my property?'

Smoke just shrugged. 'Fine. Have it your way. But just ask yourself one thing. What's more important? You or her? And if it's her, then you'll know what to do.'

That was another thing I didn't want to hear, but it stayed in my head long after he'd gone and I was alone, echoing and bouncing around in my skull like a pinball in a machine.

Who's more important? Me or her?

What the fuck did that even mean?

Give me a beer, give me pussy, give me my bike and a whole stretch of freeway, those were the things that were simple and uncomplicated. Things that I could count on to make me feel better. Those were the things I could trust. They never kicked me over and over again like this feeling was. They never made me hurt.

I tried to concentrate on the bikes for a couple of hours afterwards, but nothing seemed to work. I couldn't stop thinking about Summer. About how she'd left. How she'd looked me straight in the eye and told me I had to let her go. Even when I'd snarled at her, she hadn't been afraid. She'd been calm and certain and sure.

It was only at the end that I'd seen something like fear light in her eyes. When she'd tried to explain herself. But I hadn't wanted to listen. She was just like Mom, leaving me with some bullshit excuses. And that was fine, I'd deal, just like I dealt with everything.

But you're not dealing. So why the fuck did you let her go?

I had no answer to that, though I suspected it was there inside me, sitting somewhere I didn't want to see it.

I tried to distract myself with TV and then looking through my bike mags, but nothing worked. I couldn't sit still, couldn't relax.

I wanted Summer so badly it was agony.

So stop being a sulky little bitch and go get her.

Fuck, I'd never had a problem before with going out and taking what I wanted. What the hell was my deal now?

What's more important?

Smoke's voice echoed in my head all of a sudden

and I froze midpace, the meaning of the question abruptly hitting me hard over the back of my head.

She was more important, no question. She was so fucking smart, so fucking bright and beautiful. She had everything going for her, a new job and a new life. There was no room in that life for a dumbass like me. An illiterate biker with no education, whose only skill was putting together engines. What on earth would she want with that?

There wasn't one single thing about me—apart from sex—that she'd want. That she would need.

Nothing except the fact that I loved her.

And if there was one thing that Summer Grant needed it was love. She hadn't had it from her mom or her dad, or from her violent brother.

She hadn't had it from anyone. And she deserved it. She deserved every fucking bit of love I had.

She was more important. More important than this pissy fear that she wouldn't want me, that she'd walk away from me the way Mom had.

She was more important than I was.

Which meant I had to suck up this stupid fucking fear of mine and go out and tell her how I felt. How I loved her, how I didn't want to leave her. How I'd do anything in the world for her, anything at all.

She might not want that shit, but she might. And if there was even one chance she would…

I was halfway to the door of the warehouse, all ready to go after her, when someone knocked, and I wondered who the fuck it could be. And then I didn't care because whoever it was could get fucked, because I was going to go get Summer and this time I wasn't going to let anyone stand in my way.

I reached for the door and then flung it open.

And found Summer standing on the other side.

She was in jeans this time, but she was still wearing my T-shirt, and her hair was loose and falling all silky and pale down her back. She had a backpack slung over one shoulder and her blue eyes were gazing at me all wide and dark and vulnerable.

My entire body rang like a fucking bell.

'Can I come in?' Her mouth was fragile, that fucking honesty of hers written all over her face. 'There's something I want to say to you.'

I couldn't believe it. I couldn't believe she was here.

I gripped the doorframe, white-knuckled. 'I thought you didn't want to come back.'

'I know.' That gorgeous lower lip of hers trembled. 'I was wrong.'

Something squeezed hard around my heart. 'You cross this threshold, you're mine,' I said, not taking my gaze from hers, making sure she was absolutely clear. 'I let you go once. I'm not doing it again.'

Colour washed over her face and I saw relief in her big blue eyes.

And she didn't say another word. She simply walked through my door as if she couldn't think of anything she'd like better.

The fist around my heart squeezed tighter as she came in, and I shut the door after her, turning to face her.

She let her backpack slip onto the ground and

she was staring at me, her pulse frantic at the base of her throat.

I took a step towards her, wanting to touch her so badly I ached, but she held up a hand, stopping me in my tracks. 'W-wait,' she stuttered. 'I just want to say something. So, I went to my dad. And I basically told him he was to leave you alone and that if he didn't, he'd never see me again.' She swallowed. 'Then I told him I was going to the West Coast and my new job, whether he liked it or not, and that he couldn't stop me.'

'Summer, I—'

'No, I haven't finished. He didn't like it. He told me that the reason Mom never came back to me was because he had threatened her. He told her he'd take me away where she could never find me.'

That bastard. That *fucking* bastard.

But Summer went on before I could say anything. 'I think that was the moment I finally realised that he wasn't scary. He was just a bitter old man who was afraid and trying to get power any way he could.' She took a quick breath. 'He was weak, Tiger. And I was stronger than he was. Anyway, long story short. He won't be bothering you. Keep told him you were the one who brought me in anyway, so there's no drama with the club.' She was talking very fast, like she had to get it all out at once. 'But the main thing is… God, this is hard… I lied. I lied when I told you I didn't want to come back to you. Because I did. I wanted to come back and I…I was afraid that if I did, I'd never want to leave. And then you'd get sick of me—'

'Summer—'

'No. Let me finish.' Her voice was thick and there was a glitter in her blue eyes. But she straightened her spine, threw back her shoulders, looked straight at me. 'I left because I was afraid. And I want you to know that I'm not afraid any more. I know what's important now. And it's you, Tiger. It's you.'

The fist around my heart released all of a sudden and I couldn't hold back any longer. I swept her up into my arms and held her close, feeling her long, slender body shake against mine. 'You brave little idiot. Don't you know that I'm never going to get sick of you?' I said, holding her as I carried her over to the couch. 'What's mine stays mine. And you're mine, baby girl. You were mine the moment I took you out of the clubhouse.'

'Oh, Tiger.' She wrapped her arms around my neck and pressed her face to my throat, her voice going all muffled. 'I'm so sorry I lied. I was scared. I couldn't see how you'd want someone like me—'

'Shush.' I sat down on the couch, everything inside me suddenly loose and easy, like a rusty engine finally being oiled. Then I arranged her in my lap with her head on my shoulder, so I could look down into her slightly reddened eyes. 'You're the smartest person I know. Plus you're the bravest and the strongest. You stood up to your dad. You stood up to me. You don't take any of my shit and I respect the hell out of that. Not to mention the fact that you're the most beautiful thing I've ever seen. Fuck, you light up this place like the sun.'

She blinked, her mouth going all vulnerable again. 'Really? You really think that about me?'

'Yeah, I really do. I don't know what the hell you'd want with a dumbass like me—'

'You're not a dumbass!' She looked fierce. 'No one else gets me when I talk math, but you do. We think the same way, Tiger. And you're smart. You're probably as smart as I am.'

I shook my head, trying to ignore how much I loved hearing her say that to me. 'I dunno if that's true.'

'It *is* true.'

'You're fierce, baby girl. You're going to give me a big head.'

'Good.' She looked very serious all of a sudden. 'Look, I don't need to go to Silicon Valley. I'll stay here, find something else. I don't care what. As long as I'm with you, it doesn't matter—'

I put a finger on her lovely mouth, silencing her. 'Oh, hell, no. You're not giving up that job.' She began to protest, but I pressed my finger harder. 'Quiet, I haven't finished. I'm going to come with you to the West Coast.' Her lips moved beneath my finger, but I kept it right where it was. 'You need that job, Summer. Like I already told you, you're so fucking smart and you deserve every fucking chance, and you're taking it, end of story.'

Her eyes were very wide and full of questions, so I let my finger slide away. 'But what about the club?' she demanded instantly. 'I know how important that is to you. You can't give that up for me.'

'Bullshit I can't. I'll go nomad. Which means I'll be a kind of a scout for the club, send back intel, that kind of shit. Hell, maybe I'll even think about setting up a new chapter. In the meantime, I can set up a workshop if I want. I can work on bikes anywhere. But the important thing is that I want to be with you. And if that's what I have to do, then I'll do it.'

'But, Tiger—'

'That's not your choice, baby girl. It's mine.'

She let out a sigh, then finally gave a tiny nod.

I tightened my arms around her. 'But there's two things you're going to do for me in return.'

That lovely mouth of hers curved. 'No problem. Especially if it's something to do with sex.'

I grinned. 'I love your enthusiasm, baby, but it's not about sex. First, you're going to teach me how to read, and second, you're going to help me find my mom and little brother.'

Her big blue eyes sparkled. 'Are you sure about this? Are you absolutely, completely sure?'

'I've never been surer of anything in my entire life.' The words were nothing but the truth.

She leaned up then, kissing me, her mouth so soft and sweet. 'I love you,' she whispered. 'That's the main reason I came back. Because I love you and you needed someone to come back to you.'

My heart, that fucking piece of crap, swelled up like a balloon in my chest. 'You know, I was on my way out, just as you knocked.'

'Oh? Where were you going?'

I stared into her eyes. 'To find you.'

She went pink. 'Why?'

'Why do you think? I haven't got much to give you, not for everything you've given me. But my heart is yours if you want it.'

Her blue eyes got even bluer, even deeper. 'You idiot. That's all I've wanted since I was seventeen years old.'

I blinked like the dumbass I was, and then she kissed me again, harder. 'I always had a thing for bad boys,' she went on. 'Particularly ones who like engines and puzzles, and who don't find math boring. And have the highest sex IQ of anyone I know.'

Fuck, she always knew just what to say. 'I think I love you, baby girl.'

'I think that might be my magic pussy.'

I laughed, then I picked her up in my arms and carried her upstairs.

And we made a little magic.

Together.

EPILOGUE

Summer

CAT AND SMOKE took us out to the airport, but I was
nervous. Not because I thought Tiger might have
second thoughts, but because I was afraid he might
regret his decision. Because he wasn't just saying
goodbye to his club, but to his family, as well.

We were both a little red-eyed from the party at
the clubhouse the night before, both a goodbye party
and a public claiming where he made me his old lady
in front of his brothers. It had been scary and thrilling, though Tiger had insisted on taking me back to
his place before anything had got too wild. Which
I was slightly disappointed about. But only slightly.
Mainly because I loved him being possessive of me
and couldn't get enough of it.

This morning was no different and he kept his
arm around me the whole way through check-in.

But I had tears in my eyes when he said goodbye
to Smoke, a manly hug and that was it. Then Smoke
raised a brow, glanced at me and then back at Tiger

'Guess you found the answer, huh?' he asked cryptically.

Tiger smiled. 'Yeah. Don't worry. Your position as love guru is safe.'

Smoke grinned, pulling Cat tighter against him. She glanced at me and rolled her eyes, which made me laugh.

'I'll see you round,' Tiger said. 'Hey, maybe I'll even write.'

Smoke's grin became wider. 'You do that.'

And that was that.

Tiger didn't let me go as we walked through security and he didn't look back. 'Here's to the future, baby girl,' he murmured in my ear. 'It's gonna be great.'

* * * * *

COMING SOON!

We really hope you enjoyed reading this book. If you're looking for more romance, be sure to head to the shops when new books are available on

Thursday
26th July

LET'S TALK
Romance

For exclusive extracts, competitions
and special offers, find us online:

f facebook.com/millsandboon

◎ @millsandboonuk

🐦 @millsandboon

Or get in touch on 0844 844 1351*

For all the latest titles coming soon, visit
millsandboon.co.uk/nextmonth